CW00552265

Praise for Dan and Robert Zangari

"Dan Zangari and Robert Zangari have crafted a superb opening epic to what promises to be a deeply involved and dedicated fantasy series."

—K.C. Finn, Readers' Favorite

"A solid story told in the tradition of older fantasy novels."

— 28th Annual Writer's Digest Self-Published Book Awards

"Absolutely fantastic! [In *A Prince's Errand*] you get those hints of the *Wheel of Time*—that huge epic scale Robert Jordan really tried to produce. You get that sense of majesty with the books that Brandon Sanderson writes. There is a gritty realism to it with something like Robert E. Howard, with threads of David Eddings... [*A Prince's Errand*] is a beautiful, beautiful piece of passion. If you're looking to pick up a book that will keep you hooked for a long, long time, make sure to get this book."

—Cameron Day, Comics, Clerics, & Controllers

"*A Prince's Errand* is an intricately crafted tale of high fantasy that is as rich in detail as it is in entertainment."

—Michael Cole, Design Wizard Blog: Top 50 Wattpad Books of 2018

BY **DAN ZANGARI & ROBERT ZANGARI**
PUBLISHED BY LOK PUBLISHING

TALES OF THE AMULET
A Prince's Errand · I

TALES OF THE AMULET: COMPANION STORIES
A Thief's Way

PREQUEL NOVELS
The Prisoner of Tardalim

Beneath the Frozen Wastes

Coming Soon...
TALES OF THE AMULET
The Dark Necromancer · II
Elven Secrets · III
The Mages' Agenda · IV
Treachery in the Kingdom · V
The Red Ruby · VI

PREQUEL NOVELS
Fall of the Elves
Extinction of the Lish'sha

TALES OF THE AMULET: COMPANION STORIES
The Last Barsionist
Mysterious Assassin
Return of the Elves
A Forgotten Hero
Guardians of Kalda

DAN ZANGARI &
ROBERT ZANGARI

BENEATH THE FROZEN WASTES

An Untold Tales of Kalda Story

LOK
PUBLISHING

A LOK PUBLISHING BOOK • SALT LAKE CITY

LEGENDS OF KALDA®

Tales of the Amulet

BENEATH THE FROZEN WASTES

Hardcover Edition

Cover Art by Kerem Beyit
Chapter Heading Illustrations by Suleyman Temiz
Cartography by Robert Zangari

Edited by Linda Branam

First Printing: April 27th, 2021

ISBN 10-digit: 1-947673-16-5

ISBN 13- digit: 978-1-947673-16-8

Visit our web site at www.legendsofkalda.com

CONTENTS

For Lumpy,

You crazy, crazy lump

You remind me

Of old Amendal trying to talk

Through a gosset…

Bradisar

CARDA WASTES
(Terrain Unknown)

Duras

COMDOLITH

THE BLACK MOUNTAINS
Crindor
HIGH VALLEY

ISLE OF

Kardorth
Cordan
Karthar **MALTIN**

THE ELVEN REALM
CORDATH
Mitvrn

Merath *(Topography Estimated)*
New Sorjin

KILDATH

TILSANA GULF
LITOR
Kildath

Litlim
LOSIAN GULF

SEA OF
KORATH

TURBULANT SEA
KALADORN
KERINDOR
Los

Estrom
Kerlaris
Alath

GASTRIM

Gastrim
KINGDOM OF LOS

WESTERN SOVEREIGNTY
HENDEN
Arbath

Tor
Monddar
Henden
MELAR FOREST

MINDOLARN EMPIRE
KLIS
Klath

Mindolarn
Klis

Korum

ALGIN GULF
Hilarn

HOLORUM
DENDRIM ISLES

KALISHIR OCEAN
ISLE OF
MERDAN
CANTIE

Keth
CANTIR ISLES

NEMDAR ISLANDS

PRINCIPALITY OF SOROTH

The W
(ANOM

Soroth
UNITED ISLES OF DAMNIR

ABODINE
WASTELAND

KALDA

CIRCA 6,793 C.D.

10 20 30 40 50 60 70 80 90 100
Length in Hundred Grand Phineals

Nyesil

THE FORSAKEN LANDS OF
AZRIN'II

Xilarim   Osivir   DESERT OF
DALISIN   ASH
CONFEDERACY

Dalistim

SILRLAIN OCEAN   OCEAN OF TEMPESTS

Veir   Bithiar
ACHEYLON   ICEACEAN SEA

Arithan

RUINED KINGDOMS OF
KRESH'DAL

THE FORBIDDEN LANDS

DESOLATE LANDS

SEA OF SAND

Pegalian Peninsula

PEGALIC SEA

ABODAL

CIRCA 6,437 C.D.

10 20 30 40 50 60 70 80

Length in Hundred Grand Phineals

The World's Frown
Chameleon's Corridor

RUINED KINGDOMS OF KRESH'DAL
(The Forsaken Lands)

Aloria Gulf

Voraj'na

Arith'onge

ESHARIAN COLLECTIVE

Mavritar

Elar'inan

Wira'arim

Varquha

Lake Vadista

Tirabis'ocul

Ultra

Falchtar

Talstan Ice Shelf

Talabis'uruo

Dazali

Lake Nahan

Darzalina

R'emaniel

Handasa

Qarathnia

NARSHAR PLAINS

Emmc'eal

Tarant Mountains

Elgar Range

Tardalin

Lake Casluda

Iarodar

Vabinoold

Cahnasiard

PEGALIC SEA

KALLSETT

Talebion's Fingers

Galloria Gulf

PLAINS OF VAGON

Bal'aftilear

Fer'onhn'tel

Kalura

OCEAN

Valchtar

PRINCIPALITY OF SOROTH

Borkhiral
(The Desolate Land)

MAP KEY

- Ice Shelf Coastline
- Arctic Land Coastline
- Ocean
- Ice Shelf
- Ice Lakes and Shores
- Ice Rivers
- Arctic Land
- Non-arctic Coastline
- Mountains
- Gorges & Canyons
- ⊙ Capitols
- ○ Cities
- □ Fortresses
- ▣ Ruined or Deserted Cities
- Non-arctic Land

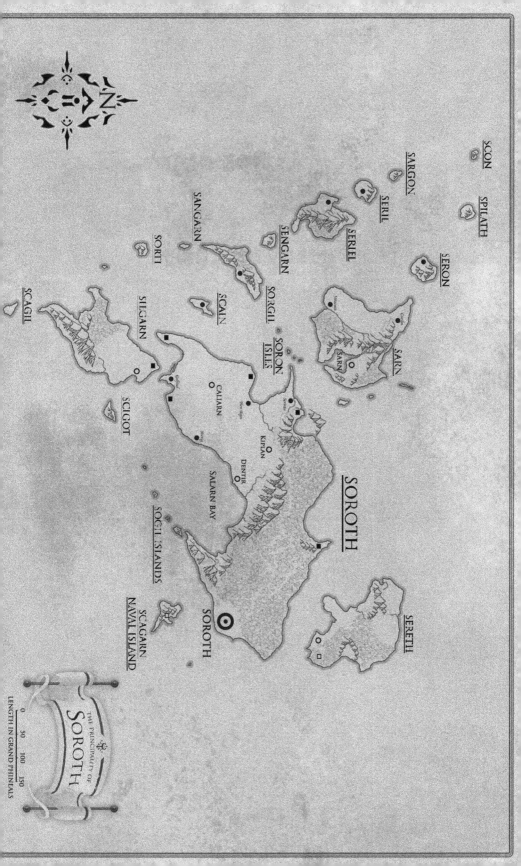

"Abodal, the true name of the Abodine Wasteland, was once home to a wondrous civilization. They thrived in the frigid climate, laid claim to the frozen plains, and built grand cities that rivaled the sprawling metropolis of Kardorth."

- From *History of the Eshari*, page 1

6,481 C.D.

The chilling wind pierced Iltar to the bone. *What a wretched place,* he thought, squinting against the icy blast. Behind him Cornar shouted orders to the others of their band, but Iltar paid little attention to the details.

Iltar pulled his thick black fur coat tightly around himself while raising a gloved hand to his graying mustache and goatee. Shivering, he gazed across the frozen plains of the Abodine Wasteland—the southernmost continent of Kalda, at the world's southern pole. He stood at the edge of his party's camp, surveying the path he and Cornar were to take. Iltar and the others of his band had trekked across this god-forsaken wasteland for the past three days, searching for rumored ruins within an icy gorge.

The rumors were in the form of a map stolen by the old thief, Cedath. Cedath had found the map while pilfering a necklace from the vault of a Sarn noblewoman. Once the map was in his possession, Cedath promptly delivered the map to Iltar and Cornar.

After considering the map—and the dangers of the Wastes—Iltar and Cornar held a council with their band's other leaders.

When Amendal Aramien saw the map, the conjurer beamed with exuberant anticipation. Amendal *demanded* that they go in search of these ruins, since the Abodine Wasteland held the greatest wonders of the world—or so the crazed fool claimed. Amendal insisted that they were bound to discover tevisrals—objects capable of channeling magic. That piqued the interest of the other leaders. They took a vote, and though they were not all as enthusiastic as Amendal, they all agreed.

Iltar and the others set sail soon after, chartering Captain Kenard's ship, the *White Duchess*.

Once they landed on the icy shores, they set out immediately. Amendal and the other conjurers had tried using conjured birds to scout ahead, but most of the fowl died from the bitter cold. The party's illusionists—including Iltar—had also sent their illusions to scour the wastes, but they found nothing but snow and ice. So Cornar decided they should divide the band into groups of three—two warriors to one mage—and search in a fanning pattern, as they normally did.

Another gust of wind pushed against Iltar and he groaned, rubbing his chest in an attempt to keep warm. *We better find these ruins soon.*

Snow crunched behind him, and he glanced over his shoulder. Cornar plodded toward him with Dugan, the other member of their party. Both warriors wore chain mail beneath their thick dark-brown coats.

Almost like burly bears, he mused. Cornar looked bearish enough even without the extra padding. Iltar's lips twitched in a bemused grin. *Beside him, I look like an aging panther.*

When Cornar reached Iltar's side, his deep emerald eyes met Iltar's gaze. "Are you ready to go?" Cornar asked, his breath frosting the thick brown beard he'd grown in the two weeks since they'd left Soroth.

Iltar nodded curtly, still rubbing his chest

Cornar grinned, then patted Iltar on the shoulder. "Well, let's get going. The sooner we find these ruins the sooner we can keep warm."

2

TRAVERSING THE
FROZEN PLAIN

*"They called themselves the Eshari. And they were unlike
any other race of our world. For them the frigid wasteland
was a paradise."*

- From *History of the Eshari*, page 2

The wind did not let up in the slightest. Iltar had
since pulled his scarf up to his hawk-like nose, but
it did little to stave off the cold. *I should have brought
a hat*, he thought. The hood of his coat did little to retain
any warmth. His short cropped hair didn't help either.

"How much farther are we going to go?" Dugan asked.

"Let's see what's over this next drift," Cornar called,
pulling a forearm-length metal stake from his pack. The
stake had a lightstone fastened to one end that glowed a
red hue.

While Cornar placed the stake as a marker, Iltar glanced
back from whence they had come. Two markers were
barely visible in the distance; one purple and one green.

Iltar turned, searching the horizon. None of the other groups were visible. They were too far apart now. For most of the march they had been able to see the other trios. Kalder's group was the last Iltar had seen, but he hadn't seen them for some time.

"There," Cornar said, rising from the ground and striding toward the snowdrift.

Dugan shivered, rubbing his chest while glancing to Iltar. "Are you sure you can't use your magic to do anything about this cold?" the warrior asked, looking hopeful. "Maybe a barsion barrier or something?"

Iltar raised an eyebrow at Dugan. True, Iltar was a mage. He was trained as an illusionist and a necromancer, though his abilities in the magical arts were far greater than either of those disciplines. Some might consider Iltar a grand mage—a type of mage that had gained mastery over all the Channels of Magic. But Iltar didn't consider himself that adept.

He was, however, quite proficient with creating barsion barriers in fused with destructive magics. Barsion magic was used to create barriers to counteract other magical effects or negate physical forces. The barriers could also be inverted and used to restrain or trap an individual or object.

"Couldn't it just negate the cold?" Dugan asked. "Barsions negate everything else..."

"I would have to encase you completely," Iltar replied. "Otherwise it would be just like an umbrella. And I can't encase you in any of the barsion spells I know. Too dangerous"—a spike of chill struck Iltar, making his teeth chatter—"and if we happened to be on a sheet of ice, my barsion would erode it, and we would fall through. Now if I knew how to cast a flaming barsion, I could create a dome above us, but my talent in the Elemental Channel of Magic is quite limited."

Dugan sighed and hurried after Cornar, who was already partway up the snowdrift.

I should have Hex help me learn more of the Elemental Channel, Iltar thought, still shivering. He kept his eyes on Cornar, who abruptly stopped atop the snowdrift. *What are you looking at, Cor?*

Dugan reached Cornar, then waved for Iltar to hurry.

I'm coming, I'm coming! Iltar groused. Then he cleared the snowdrift's crest, and his eyes widened.

A few-hundred paces away stood a rocky hill covered in snow and ice. Icicles and sheets of ice surrounded the mouth of a cave nearly the size of a large house. The cave's mouth was offset, as if something had burrowed the opening at a shallow angle. A narrow valley lay between them and the cave, a lower elevation than the plains they had crossed.

"What do you say, Cor?" Dugan asked. "Can we set up camp here tonight?"

"That might be wise, if any of the others don't find the ruins," Cornar said. "Let's see if that cave is safe. But I'll move the marker first. I want to be able to see it from the cave's mouth." Cornar turned and hurried back down the snowdrift.

Dugan, however, started toward the cave.

"Dugan, wait!" Iltar shouted, but the warrior didn't slow. The frigid temperature was undoubtedly dulling the man's senses. "Dugan!"

Cornar returned a moment later. He glanced at Iltar then hurried after Dugan without a word.

Mindless warriors, Iltar thought, carefully descending the snowdrift. Cornar and Dugan were already halfway to the cave when Iltar reached the small valley. He ran after them, cursing to himself. The wind picked up as Iltar neared the cave, whipping across the opening and creating an eerie howl.

Ominous.

To Iltar's surprise, the warriors waited for him at the cave's mouth. Dugan stood near a waist-high icicle protruding from the ground.

"... but it's a good ten phineals away from the top." Dugan pointed to the upper parts of the cave opening. "There's nothing above it, so how could it have formed?"

Iltar slowed as he approached the perplexed warrior. The icicle Dugan was examining had sharp edges and was a transparent pale blue. It looked more like crystal than ice. Iltar also noted the distance between the icicle and the top of the cave's mouth. They were a good five or six paces apart.

Curious, Iltar thought, glancing to the cave's walls. They too were a transparent pale blue. Iltar expected to see a rocky wall that matched the hill, but the entire cavern— from what he could see—was a pale, transparent blue. The cavern's floor descended at a shallow angle, but disappeared around a bend in the cave.

Cornar stood near the center of the cave opening, cautiously studying it. "Something burrowed this," the warrior said.

Iltar crept to Cornar, and both of them continued staring into the cave. Though the sunlight spilled only partway beyond the opening, the entire cavern was brightly illuminated. It was as if the sunlight was trapped within the cavern's walls. The odd illumination spread even into that bend in the cave.

"Well, are we going inside?" Dugan demanded. "I'm cold."

"We're all cold," Iltar said, stifling a snarl.

"Follow me," Cornar said warily. His hands hovered near the hilts of his two weapons: a serrated dagger and a short-sword.

Dugan, however, drew his own weapons; a spiked mace and a sword-breaker.

Together, the three of them descended into the cave side by side. They rounded the corner, finding the cave still illuminated. The snow covering the cavern's floor lessened, revealing a crystalline surface as brightly lit as the walls.

This cave can't be covered in ice, Iltar thought, glancing to the glowing floor. But it couldn't be crystal either. He didn't know of any crystal that retained or gave off light. At least, not any natural crystal.

3

INTO THE CAVE

"It is unclear when exactly the Eshari colonized Abodal. But their earliest records predate the Thousand Years War."

- From *History of the Eshari*, page 2

W
e need to be careful," Iltar whispered.

Cornar shot him a grin. "I'm always careful, my friend."

"Extra careful," Iltar said through clenched teeth. "This cave wasn't burrowed by anything natural."

"So you don't think this is ice?" Dugan asked, pointing to the crystalline wall.

Iltar shook his head.

"What kind of beast burrowed this then?" Cornar asked.

"Uh," Dugan muttered, "you don't suppose there is a monster in here... do you?"

Iltar set his jaw, remembering a particular creature that could turn whatever it touched to crystal. Of course, the beast was mythological. But Iltar knew better than to discount myth when facing potential threats.

"Iltar?" Cornar asked.

Sighing, Iltar studied the tunnel once again before answering. "There is an obscure tale about a being that could change whatever it touched into a substance resembling crystal, a crysillac. They are said to be monstrously huge." He paused, waving at the cave around them. "About the size of this tunnel. They are long, snake-like beings with insect-like legs."

Dugan swallowed hard.

"I don't suppose anyone has ever seen one of these... *crysillacs?*" Cornar asked. "Has Amendal ever mentioned it?"

Iltar shook his head.

Cornar immediately drew his weapons. Both the serrated dagger and short-sword gleamed with pale-blue light, as if they had absorbed magic. Many times Iltar had imbued Cornar's weapons with destructive power. Those blades held onto the magic even through a dispel. They were curious weapons.

Iltar glanced to Dugan's sword breaker, which only reflected the cavern's light. *Odd*, he thought, turning back to Cornar.

These walls aren't crystals either, Iltar thought, stepping away from the warriors. He moved to the left side of the cavern, extending his hand toward the strange wall. A faint tingle brushed against his fingertips. He reached closer to the wall, and the tingling grew to a constant surge. *Interesting...*

"Cor, come here," Iltar said, eyes still fixed on the cavern wall.

Cornar complied, briefly studying Iltar. He smiled with

enlightenment, then shoved his dagger toward the cavern wall. The crystalline substance stopped the blade, but the metal gleamed brighter than before.

"Whoa!" Dugan exclaimed.

Iltar nodded. "So, it is magic…"

Cornar pulled his dagger back, examining the blade. "What kind of magic is this?" he asked. "It looks like barsion, plain barsion."

"It's not," Iltar said. "I don't know what it is…"

"Um, isn't all magic supposed to be identifiable by color?" Dugan asked.

"When properly channeled," Iltar said. "This… this is raw." Many scholars of the magical arts speculated that magic in its raw, unchanneled form did not match the color it bore when manifested by a mage or tevisral. But Iltar hadn't known of any being that could manifest magic in its raw form. The whole idea of raw magic was rather speculative and based on ancient texts whose validity was questionable.

"Let's continue through this tunnel," Cornar said, turning from the cavern wall.

4

TRESPASSERS

"The Eshari tamed many of Abodal's beasts: the cisthyrn, the yaeltis, and the vaerym. These were deadly creatures, but their lethality paled in comparison to the crysillac."

- From *History of the Eshari*, page 5

Iltar and the warriors continued silently through the cave. The temperature inside was a little warmer than the frozen plains, but not by much. The light from the walls grew brighter the farther they went. Besides their footsteps, the cave was deathly silent.

After what seemed like an hour, they arrived at a crude intersection of tunnels, each as large as the first.

"Which way do we go?" Dugan asked.

Cornar pointed his serrated dagger to the tunnel straight ahead of them and continued in that direction.

Iltar followed, remaining just as quiet as Cornar. Many of their adventures over the years had required significant stealth.

This new tunnel twisted and turned several times. As

Iltar and the others rounded a bend, faint clicking echoed off the walls.

Dugan shot Iltar a surprised glance and gripped his weapons more tightly while halting.

Cornar continued to press forward without hesitation. He was the type of man that would run headlong into danger, mostly to draw the attention of that danger from those around him. But he wasn't a fool. He would consider the risk, but that consideration would last less than a heartbeat.

Iltar was often right beside Cornar during those charges. He couldn't let his friend face those perils alone. And this instance was no different. Grinning, Iltar thought, *If I let Cor take all the glory it might go to his head.*

The clicking noises grew louder the farther they pressed into the tunnel.

Soon, the tunnel turned and emptied into an enormous cavern. A small village, stacked many times over, could fit inside the vast space. At first glance, Iltar supposed the cave's ceiling rose nearly ten stories.

Iltar and the warriors halted, and Dugan stifled a gasp. The three men stared in awe at a gigantic creature that matched the obscure myth of the crysillac

From what Iltar could tell, the crysillac was as long as a city block. It was as tall and wide as the tunnels they had traversed. The beast circled the center of the cavern, slithering on its belly, despite the hundreds of insect-like legs protruding from the pale-gold colored carapace that encased much of its body. Why was it slithering? Those chitinous legs, tipped with pincers, slid limply along the cavern floor, the pincers clicking noisily. Transparent pale blue tentacles as tall as the cave, lined the creature's back, sweeping across the cavern's ceiling. Each tentacle pulsed a pale blue—its light matching the color of the cavern.

The crysillac's body tapered to an odd tail that split in two. The tail's two ends were longer than the tentacles on the creature's back. They also glowed a pale blue, though the tails weren't transparent.

"Uh, we should go…" Dugan muttered, stepping back into the tunnel.

Iltar glanced to Cornar, but as their eyes met, the clicking ceased.

Stealing his nerves, Iltar turned to face the crysillac.

The beast had stopped its slithering. The crysillac stood upon its many legs, raising its head. An oblong face towered above the snake-like body, with an octagonal orifice large enough to swallow Iltar and the other two men whole. Sharp fangs, each as long as a man was tall, lined the corners of its bizarre mouth. The fangs were not fixed like teeth. Eight red eyes surrounded the mouth, offset between each of the fangs. More tentacles were arrayed around the head, dancing through the air.

Crab-like claws lined the forward parts of the crysillac, arrayed like arms. It had six of those claws, three along each side.

The crysillac stared at Iltar and the warriors. It blinked once, a transparent film briefly covering its red eyes.

"Looks like it's not a myth after all," Cornar whispered, his tone calm.

"What are you two waiting for?" Dugan muttered. "We *need* to get out of here!"

Iltar looked back to Cornar, then to the monster. The

creature didn't move. It was just staring at them. The beast was probably as perplexed as Iltar and the others. It had most likely never encountered men.

"Well?" Dugan demanded.

Iltar held a hand out to quiet the wary warrior.

At Iltar's gesture, the crysillac turned, scurrying out of the cavern through another tunnel. It barely fit through the opening, its tentacles pressing against the tunnel's walls and ceiling. The crysillac soon disappeared, leaving behind a cacophony of clicking that rang through the enormous cave.

"Strange..." Cornar whispered.

"What just happened?" Dugan demanded.

"I don't know..." Iltar said, squinting at the tunnel where the monster had fled. *Where did it go?* he wondered, turning back to where the crysillac had been circling. That part of the cavern floor looked like a shallow bowl. *Had it been burrowing a new tunnel?*

A tug at Iltar's arm drew his attention. He turned, facing Cornar. The warrior placed his gloved hand on Iltar's shoulder.

"Enhance us," Cornar said flatly, his emotions bridled.

Iltar complied, uttering an incantation. White particles of magic flowed from his hands, encircling him and the two warriors. The magic surged through each of them, quickening their reflexes, enhancing their stamina, and increasing their physical capabilities.

"I'm glad you came to your senses, Cor," Dugan said.

Cornar shot the other warrior a rebuking glance. "Now our weapons, Iltar."

"What?!" Dugan blurted. "You... you don't want to

hunt that thing, do you?"

"No," Cornar replied, "but if it attacks us I want to be prepared. Who knows how this monster will react to us intruding on its territory. For all we know, it might be cutting off our escape right now."

The two warriors continued arguing about their situation while Iltar focused on imbuing their weapons with destructive power.

Iltar uttered another incantation, mustering acidic magic. The pale-yellow-green particles wisped to both warriors' weapons, bathing them with sickly light. He uttered another incantation, mustering a dark gray cloud. Tiny bolts of lightning surged within the cloud, then shot to the four weapons. The lightning surged across the glowing metal, mingling with the acid in an ever persistent imbuing.

With the weapons enhanced, Iltar closed his eyes. He focused his mind on a latent power nestled deep within him. He pulled that power to the surface, mentally commanding it to manifest. Manifesting this power was akin to mustering magic, but this power was accessed *without* incantation, directed by mere thought.

Black mist oozed from his hands, flowing toward both warriors' weapons. The black mist—what Iltar called the Darkness magic—could devour all it touched. He carefully guided it to both of the warriors' weapons, commanding the mist to persist around the metal.

With the warriors' weapons sufficiently enhanced, Iltar uttered an incantation. More pale-yellow-green magic shot from his hands, surrounding both warriors with an acidic veil of barsion magic. The acidic barsion would protect the men while splashing acid on anything that tried to touch them. The protective magic was corrosive enough to blunt swords and erode arrow tips.

Iltar closed his eyes again, mustering his own protection made from the Darkness magic, a barrier he called his Necrotic Sphere of Protection.

As the black mist oozed from his pores, faint clicking echoed down the tunnel he and the others had traversed.

"I knew we should have started running!" Dugan blurted.

Almost there… Iltar thought, sensing the flowing magic coalescing around him. The clicking grew louder, and Iltar opened his eyes. Both warriors dropped into battle stances while a black mist swirled around Iltar. But before the Necrotic Sphere of Protection formed, the crysillac appeared, charging straight for Iltar and the others.

5

ENTER THE
CRYSILLAC

*"For centuries the Eshari avoided the crysillacs. The beasts
burrowed caves into the heart of the wasteland, near the forbidden mountain created by the Irum'mak'sha to house the
prison of Tardalim."*

- From *History of the Eshari*, page 6

In a flash of movement, the crysillac barreled through
the tunnel, its pincers violently scraping along the
crystalline floor. The beast's face was low to the
ground, its mouth splayed as if ready to consume Iltar and
the warriors.

"Move!" Cornar shouted, dashing to the side of the
tunnel.

Jaw clenched, Iltar darted toward the other side, as did
Dugan.

Cornar evaded the monster, but the crysillac's foremost
legs collided with Iltar and Dugan. The force of the monster's advance sent both men flying. The blow sucked the
breath from Iltar—the crysillac's legs had passed through

the forming barrier and smacked Iltar's chest.

The crysillac wailed, stumbling into the enormous cavern. Its blue tentacles spread into the air, undulating in a dazzling pattern.

As Iltar skidded to a halt, his necrotic sphere of protection formed. Breathing deeply, Iltar sensed his Darkness magic surging across the monster's foremost left leg. A black mist eroded the chitinous fibers, turning them to gray dust. The Darkness soon dissipated, but not before dissolving half of the crysillac's limb.

The wailing ceased, and Cornar dashed toward the monster, swinging his weapons. The crysillac, however, saw the warrior's advance and swung one of its crab-like claws.

As acidic barsion and claw met, Cornar flew back across the cavernous lair. The crysillac howled again, acid streaming down its claw.

"That thing is too big!" Dugan blurted from beside Iltar.

Iltar shot the warrior an annoyed glance, then dashed farther into the monster's lair. As he ran, Iltar drew upon the Darkness magic. Streams of blackness wisped from his hands, forming several palm-sized orbs, condensed spheres of corrosive power. Globes of darkness, Iltar called them.

The monster ceased howling, then darted toward Cornar. The warrior had already recovered and was charging, yelling a battle cry as he ran.

Before warrior and monster clashed, Iltar threw a globe of darkness at the crysillac. The black orb shot from Iltar's protection, creating a rippling effect in the black barrier—like a fish leaping from water.

Cornar leapt unnaturally into the air, weapons poised to strike.

The crysillac lowered its mouth, ready to swallow the warrior whole.

Cornar neared the creature's gaping mouth as Iltar's globe of darkness struck the monster's face. The orb splashed across the crysillac, dissolving its flesh.

Pained, the crysillac screamed and jerked upward.

Cornar collided against its bottommost eye, grating and slicing the monster's strange face as he fell.

The crysillac thrashed wildly, shrieking.

Iltar threw another globe of darkness, and the orb struck one of the monster's tentacles.

Cornar landed gracefully, then darted toward the crysillac's legs. He swung with furious precision, his weapons cutting through the chitinous fibers.

The crysillac convulsed, then reared up to evade the warrior, but hit the ceiling. The monster shrieked again, then dove toward Cornar. It swatted at the warrior with one of its claws, flinging Cornar through the air.

Cornar sailed toward the cavern wall opposite Iltar, straight for several human-sized holes bored through the crystalline surface.

With uncanny precision, Cornar *fell* into a hole and disappeared.

"Cor!" Iltar shouted.

The crysillac took one glance at the hole where Cornar had vanished, then turned on Iltar and Dugan.

Damn beast! He glanced to the tunnel they had traversed, but the monster's tail was still blocking it. Iltar, however, couldn't run away. He couldn't abandon Cornar.

"Cor!" Iltar shouted again.

There was no reply.

The monster wailed as it settled back onto the cavern floor. It stared at Iltar in what could only be a menacing glare. The crysillac glanced to Dugan, but returned its seven-eyed gaze to Iltar. The petrified warrior was still standing where the creature had initially repulsed him.

"Come on," Iltar said, settling into a wide stance. Though he stared at the monster he focused on streaming more of the Darkness magic from his pores. The black mists coalesced, forming vague sphere-shapes.

The crysillac advanced slowly, its tentacles arcing forward.

I'll blast this thing to oblivion, Iltar thought, condensing each of the forming orbs. A burst of anger surged through him—a result of mustering the Darkness magic.

Suddenly, four of the tentacles lashed toward Iltar.

Instinctively, Iltar flung his initial globes of darkness at the tentacles. He missed two, but clipped one and severed another. The errant globes soared through the crysillac's lair, but Iltar redirected them.

The monster wailed, but the tentacles still advanced. They struck the ground beside Iltar, sliding across the crystalline floor and leaving a trail of pale-blue light. Was the monster trying to do something to the floor?

The severed tentacle landed beside Iltar, still glowing.

A force pressed against Iltar's necrotic sphere of protection, coming from the severed tentacle. He felt that force trying to transmute the corrosive particles of his barrier. All the while, the three tentacles continued sweeping around Iltar.

What is—?

The ground shook beneath him.

At that moment, a dozen globes of darkness formed around Iltar.

Still redirecting the errant orbs, Iltar struck the un-maimed tentacles, severing them like the first. They fell, landing between him and the crysillac.

The monster howled, though it didn't sound as wild as at first. Was the creature pushing through its pain?

More rumbling surged beneath Iltar and he glanced down. The crystalline floor cracked beneath his feet.

"Oh, no—"

Iltar spun, pushing off the ground to run, but the cracking floor collapsed beneath him. He fell, shards of crystal colliding with his black barrier. The shards turned to dust and wisped through the air. Iltar hit something, then tumbled down a steep slope.

"Master Iltar!" Dugan wailed, but the warrior's voice soon faded.

6
FORBIDDEN WARRENS

"Eventually, some of the Eshari tried to tame the crysillacs. Their attempts were in vain."

- From *History of the Eshari*, page 6

Iltar struggled to slow himself. His necrotic sphere of protection eroded the sloping ground, counteracting friction's negating force. Amid his tumbling, Iltar glimpsed the hole from which he had fallen. It was at least a dozen stories above him.

The slope leveled, and Iltar rolled across another crystalline floor. He threw himself sideways, staggering to his feet.

What a fall, he thought, gazing upward. The hole was small from this distance. That fall would have been fatal without his necrotic sphere of protection.

Faint screaming filtered from the hole, undoubtedly Dugan. Iltar strained his focus, attempting to discern if any of his magic was still active around the man. Mages could often *feel* where their magic was, as long as it was not too far away. Iltar sensed that the acidic barsion was gone, but the enhancing magic was still in force.

Dugan was running, moving toward the tunnel leading to the surface.

You're not going to make it, Iltar groaned inwardly, then flung his newly formed globes of darkness toward the hole in the ceiling.

Iltar blindly redirected the black orbs through the monster's lair, hoping to hit the crysillac. Some hit the cavern wall, others struck the creature, but a few missed. Iltar tried redirecting them, but only one struck the crysillac; the others hit the cavern's wall.

Horrific wails echoed from the crysillac's lair. Suddenly, Iltar no longer sensed his enhancing magic.

"Poor fool," Iltar sighed. The crysillac had probably eaten Dugan.

Still encased in his necrotic sphere of protection, Iltar turned about, trying to sense Cornar. Each of the magics around the warrior was still active, though somewhat faint. Cornar was below the monster's lair, but not as deep as Iltar. *Those holes must have been shafts of some kind*, Iltar thought. But for what? Why would a monster need shafts in its lair?

"Stay alive, Cor," Iltar whispered. "I'm coming."

Determined to find his friend, Iltar surveyed this new cavern. Its ceiling was as tall as the tunnels and spread from the hole where Iltar had fallen, branching off in several places. Like the tunnels, it was covered completely in that strange crystalline substance.

It can't be a coincidence that the monster broke the ground where I was standing, he thought. The crysillac must be fairly intelligent. It *intended* to separate him from the others.

"That thing is hunting us one by one," he whispered. *Hopefully it will come after me next.* If the monster went after Cornar the warrior would not survive.

Iltar hurried toward the branching tunnels, taking the one that he thought would lead him toward Cornar. More tunnels branched off from each other. Each was eerily silent. Iltar did his best to navigate the labyrinth. Amid his wandering, he no longer sensed the barsion protecting Cornar.

The enhancement and the destructive power on the weapons, however, still persisted.

"You better not die, Cor," Iltar grumbled, now dashing through the labyrinth. As he turned a corner, a faint repeating sound carried into the tunnel.

Iltar halted, straining his hearing.

It was breathing, deep breathing.

Cautious, Iltar continued through the tunnel. The crystalline ground thinned, as did the tunnel's walls. The illumination found elsewhere lessened, and the tunnel was dimly lit by patches of crystal. From what Iltar could tell, the *true* walls and floor of the cavern were a dark-colored stone.

Iltar crept across the stone floor, careful to not make a noise. The breathing grew louder as he pressed onward, rounding a shallow bend. Though it was dark he could see the source of the breathing.

Another crysillac.

But this one was much larger than the first. The monster was asleep and coiled like a snake, revealing its bulging belly. Tall curved spikes lined its carapace, instead of undulating tentacles. Some were barbed with glistening tines. Was this a female? Iltar knew of some creatures whose *fairer* sex was larger and more gruesome than its male counterparts.

Iltar did not move. *There has to be another way around this one*, he thought. Iltar glanced about the dark lair, but there were no other tunnels.

Perhaps I should go another way, he thought, furrowing his brow. He studied the slumbering crysillac once more, his eyes drawn to its belly. The monster looked engorged. Was it spawning more of its kind?

Iltar pushed aside the thought and hurried back through the tunnel.

*"The crysillacs were unlike any other creature native to
Abodal. While the beasts of Abodal devoured flesh, the
crysillacs consumed crystal—crystal that was produced only
by the innate abilities of the males."*

- From *History of the Eshari*, page 8

Iltar wandered for what seemed hours. He found several more large caverns like the first lair, each covered
in glistening crystal.

Throughout his searching, Iltar kept his necrotic sphere
of protection about him, despite the lack of immediate
danger. Either crysillac could be upon him in the blink of
an eye, and he didn't want to waste time trying to protect
himself.

Eventually, Iltar found a rising slope in one of the lair-
like caverns and ascended it. Once in this new set of tunnels he sensed he was on the same level as Cornar.

The destructive power on the warrior's weapons suddenly disappeared, but the enhancement remained. Cornar

was undoubtedly using his weapons against *something*—whether that be the monster or the caverns. There was no telling where those small shafts led, and Cornar could have found himself trapped in some crevasse. If that were the case, the warrior would have tried to cut his way free, using the magic of his weapons and the destructive nature of the acidic barsion.

Hang on, Cor.

Urgency swelled within Iltar as he continued wandering through the crystalline caverns. He sensed his magic growing closer.

While traversing a curving tunnel, Iltar spotted a small squared opening to his left.

Intrigued, Iltar hurried to the opening. It was a tunnel barely taller than he was. The tunnel looked more like the hallway of a building than a rocky passageway. Though its walls were smooth crystal, the rest of the tunnel looked nothing like those burrowed by the crysillacs. *How odd...* he thought. This couldn't be part of the rumored ruins, could it?

The crystallized hallway opened into a large space that resembled a room. Was that a sword lying on the ground. And... a gauntlet?

Can there be remains in there?

Iltar glanced over his shoulder. Cornar was somewhere past that curving tunnel. But if there were remains beyond the crystallized hall Iltar could use them to his advantage.

"Hang on, Cor," Iltar whispered. "I'm coming, and hopefully with reinforcements."

He hurried through the crystallized hallway. The ground was slick, and he slipped once but recovered before falling.

He soon entered the large space. It resembled a banquet room. Crystallized furniture consisting of beautiful chairs, tables, and sofas were tossed about. Cankered weapons and rusty armor lay around the transparent furniture, mingled with frozen skeletons. The armor—a mismatched bunch of plate and chain mail—were devoid of markings or insignia.

Perfect. Iltar grinned. He passed beneath a crystal chandelier, its lightstones dun-colored, exhausted by time. But the crystallized walls gave off enough light to illuminate the room.

"How many of you are there?" Iltar whispered, surveying the corpses. He counted fifteen skeletons. Over half wore armor. *The rest were probably mages,* he thought. These corpses probably belonged to some ill-fated expedition who met their demise in these caves. Had they been trapped down here? Starved to death? Surely, the crysillacs couldn't have reached them in here.

Iltar knelt beside the nearest corpse, uttering an incantation to a reanimating spell. Dark-purple light flowed from his hands and wisped to the frozen bones. The magic permeated every part of the skeleton. Iltar moved to the next corpse and repeated the incantation. Before he finished the second spell, the first skeleton picked itself off the floor.

One by one, Iltar reanimated each of the skeletons. As he moved through the room, Iltar passed the remains of other creatures. There were several long snake-like skeletons beside the human ones, each as long as a man was tall. Dull beige shells spread from the tops of those snake-like skeletons, like curved wings.

Iltar's eyes lingered on those odd remains. They looked like miniature versions of the first crysillac he encountered.

Those couldn't be infantile crysillacs, could they? he wondered. If so, had they caused the deaths of Iltar's reanimated minions? He pushed aside the question and continued raising the dead.

Once the last of the armored skeletons stood, Iltar imbued each of them with magic. Swirling acid engulfed the bones and the weapons, the pale-yellow-green light accenting the dark-purple hue of the reanimating spell.

Iltar mustered his Darkness magic and enhanced the cankered weapons further.

With that, Iltar swiftly but cautiously hurried through the room and back down the crystallized hallway. He dashed into the large tunnel, his reanimated minions trailing behind him.

8

A BEAST
TOO CLEVER

*"The Eshari studied the crysillacs for centuries. They dis-
covered that the creatures were docile, unless one trespassed
into their crystal caverns."*

- From *History of the Eshari*, page 10

Scraping noises reached Iltar's ears when he reached
a branch in the crystallized caverns. The scraping
grew louder, coming from the right.

Iltar shot a glance to the left branch, the direction where
he felt his enhancing spell. *It's coming this way*, he thought.
Better get to Cor.

He ran to the left branch, his reanimated minions trailing behind him. Cornar was closer now. Iltar felt the enhancing spell ahead and to the left. He fought the urge to
call out to the warrior, in case the crysillac heard the cry.

The tunnel turned to the left, then curved back to the
right in a wide arc.

While rounding the shallow bend, faint scraping reached
Iltar's ears. *Oh no...* Iltar bemoaned, glancing over his

shoulder.

The scraping grew louder, accompanied by rapid click-ing.

"Cor!" Iltar shouted. There was no use trying to hide now. "Cor, where are you?!"

Iltar continued running, but commanded his minions to take up ambushing positions in the curving cavern.

"Cor!"

The scraping and clicking was louder now, the crysillac was close. Too close.

Iltar stopped fifty paces from his reanimated minions and spun. He concentrated on mustering more globes of darkness while uttering a life-draining incantation.

Streams of blackness swirled around Iltar while orange light gathered between his hands. Two orange balls formed—larger than a man's head—with tiny tendrils lashing out across their surfaces. A dozen globes of dark-ness coalesced, hovering above him.

The scraping noises echoed loudly through the cavern, then the crysillac appeared. Beside the eye that Cornar had cut, another was completely eroded—dissolved by Iltar's blind assault. More of its pale-blue tentacles were missing, and parts of its right-middle claw were eroded as was some of its carapace. The crysillac, however, did not seem fazed by the wounds.

It charged directly at Iltar.

The reanimated skeletons advanced at Iltar's command, but the crysillac tore through their ranks, swatting them away as if they were annoying insects. Several of the armed skeletons, however, evaded and swung at the crysillac's legs, their slices eroding the chitinous fibers.

The crysillac screamed but its howl seemed restrained, like a battle-hardened soldier stifling their pain with clenched teeth. Red eyes glared at Iltar with unbridled hostility.

This thing is *intelligent*. The crysillac was not like the mindless creatures he had encountered across Kalda. With its colossal size and innate magical abilities, the crysillac was far more than a worthy opponent.

And it was coming for Iltar.

Pale-blue tentacles lashed forward, light surging around them.

Iltar muttered a curse under his breath as the monster advanced. It was moving too fast for him to evade.

As the crysillac closed the gap between them, Iltar unleashed the fury of his magic. A dozen black orbs flew from the necrotic sphere of protection, the ripples blurring Iltar's vision. The orange balls of life-draining magic shot forward, the tiny tendrils rapidly expanding.

The globes of darkness struck the crysillac's face as the pale-blue tentacles reached Iltar's protective barrier. Iltar felt parts of the black mist changing to tiny shards of crystal, but each was consumed by the barrier.

Iltar's life-draining magic expanded further. The tendrils wove around the crysillac's tentacles, reaching for various parts of the monster.

A deafening howl shook the cavern as the crysillac shot its foremost claws toward Iltar. The monster scooped Iltar from the ground as the life-draining tendrils latched onto it, but the creature kept charging.

Despite the destructive power of Iltar's necrotic sphere of protection, the crysillac held onto him. What could the monster possibly be thinking? The crysillac's claws eroded, but as the thick shells were consumed, the crysillac tightened its grip.

"Obstinate beast!" Iltar shouted. He sensed his life-draining magic latching onto the monster in dozens of places. He immediately began siphoning the creature's energies, hoping to debilitate it.

Iltar's hopes, however, were in vain.

The life-draining magic had little effect on the monster, and it continued its charge.

"How is that—?"

Something struck the necrotic sphere of protection behind Iltar, then the cavern abruptly narrowed. The monster no longer held him. Had the crysillac slammed him into the cavern wall?

Yes... Iltar felt the distance growing between him and his reanimated minions. Stone assailed the necrotic sphere of protection, but turned to dust. The protective barrier was burrowing a hole through the cavern wall.

I have to slow myself, Iltar thought. He could either dismiss his corrosive barsion or muster an ensnaring spell and lash it to himself and the tunnel.

Within a heartbeat, he uttered the incantation to manifest his ensnaring tentacles. As the dark-green magic illuminated his hands, the resistance behind him faded, and Iltar felt himself falling.

9

THE RAVINE

"Mated crysillacs usually stayed in one place for most of their lives. Once they reached maturity, a male and a female would pair, then cross the frozen wasteland in search of rocky terrain. After they found a suitable spot, the male would immediately begin burrowing."

- From *History of the Eshari*, page 11

Frantic, Iltar looked about as he fell. He was no longer in that tiny opening, nor was he in the crystalline caverns.

To his surprise, Iltar was falling along a sheer cliff of dark rock. He glanced over his shoulder. The snow-covered ground raced toward him.

Heart thumping, Iltar scanned his surroundings. He was falling into a ravine, a deep ravine.

The last of the incantation left Iltar's lips, and a dark-green mass coalesced in his right hand. Through his mental focus, Iltar shot the spell in two directions. A dark-green, vine-like tentacle shot to his waist and wrapped around him while another raced to the rocky cliff side.

Both tentacles adhered to him and the rock wall in unison, abruptly stopping Iltar's fatal descent. The force of the fall, however, slammed Iltar into the rock wall. His necrotic sphere of protection hollowed out a round niche, and Iltar immediately dismissed the destructive barsion. He hit the back of the newly carved niche, then swung back out over the ravine.

A frigid wind struck his face as he swung back and forth like a pendulum. Growling, Iltar slowed the swinging with his ensnaring spell.

Sometimes the necrotic sphere is more trouble than it's worth, Iltar thought, shaking his head and breathing heavily.

Sunlight pierced the sparse clouds, lighting the ravine. It was several city blocks wide and ran to the horizon. It looked as deep as most mountains were tall. The snow-covered ground was two or three stories below him.

"That was close," he muttered. Even with his necrotic sphere of protection, that fall would have caused some injury.

A savage gust whipped through the ravine, interrupting Iltar's reverie. The gust swayed Iltar, and he shivered despite his warm clothing.

I have to get to Cor, he thought, glancing up the rock wall in search of the hole from which he had fallen. The hole, however, was not visible.

Brow furrowed, Iltar concentrated on sensing his magic. He could feel the battle still raging between the crysillac and the reanimated skeletons, but they were far away, perhaps two-thirds or three-quarters up the wall above him. His stomach churned. He didn't dare try to guess how many stories he would have to climb in order to get back to Cornar.

Iltar hung there for a moment, focused on the battle. The skeletons were still attacking, per his order. Reanimated minions did not require step-by-step manipulation, though a necromancer could control each movement if desired. Iltar found such control tedious, especially during battle. Besides, such manipulation would exhaust him, especially if he were continually mustering the Darkness magic.

The crysillac swatted each of the minions away, but the skeletons recovered and advanced on the beast. Some magic imbued into the cankered weapons had faded, exhausted from repeated blows against the crysillac.

"Well, I better start climbing," Iltar muttered.

He focused his ensnaring spell in a third direction, and another vine-like tentacle flew from his hand and lashed onto the rocky wall. Iltar used the spell to pull himself up the ravine, then detached the first tentacle and threw it to a higher spot along the cliff. All the while, the battle with the crysillac continued.

Iltar was halfway up the ravine when the acidic magic around his reanimated minions dissipated. The Darkness magic also vanished from the skeletons.

Despite its wounds, the crysillac continued fighting. The monster pummeled the skeletons with its claws, but the reanimated minions recovered. Iltar sensed the monster using its pale-blue tentacles, but the transmutative power did nothing to disrupt the necrotic bond.

Suddenly, the monster fled, darting away from the skeletons.

Odd, Iltar thought. His reanimated minions chased after the crysillac, but Iltar commanded them to halt their pursuit.

Why had it fled? Did the crysillac somehow sense the futility of attacking the reanimated skeletons?

Iltar mused on the reasons for the monster's retreat as he climbed, but soon put aside the speculation about the crysillac and stared across the ravine. Was this icy gorge the site of the ruins? *I wonder if any of the other groups have found the ruins yet.* Iltar looked to his right, the direction where the rest of the party was headed. If they hadn't discovered the ruins, then each of the trios would have returned to camp.

Surely, the day's search will be over by now, he thought, glancing at the sun. It was impossible to know how much time had passed since they had entered the crystalline caves. At this time of year in the Abodine Wasteland, the sun hung in the sky almost all day. For a short time it dipped below the horizon, but darkness lasted an hour, perhaps less.

However, both of Kalda's moons—Kistern and Kaelyrn—were visible through the clouds. If Iltar were home in Soroth, it would undoubtedly be nighttime. After all, he had spent a considerable amount of time wandering the crystal labyrinth. The others *would* have made it back to camp.

Hopefully I can find Cor before the others make their way here, Iltar thought.

Prior to landing on the icy continent, the entire band had decided they would go after anyone who might become lost in the frozen wasteland. That was why Cornar constructed the markers. Not only were they to help groups navigate back to camp, they would give the main party a general area of where to search for missing groups. Cornar was adamant about not leaving anyone behind. If a trio were to go missing during their scouting, Cornar intended to rescue them.

Ironic that we're the ones in need of rescuing, Iltar thought, looking again to his right.

Far across the ravine, a faint glint of light shone above the cliffs, shining brighter than sunlight—only magic or lightstones did that. Intrigued, Iltar continued up the rock wall. The light shone from atop a tall pale-blue shape protruding above the ravine. *Could that be the ruins?*

Still focused across the ravine, Iltar sensed his reanimated minions nearing. He turned back to the rock wall and spotted the hole where he had fallen.

With relief, Iltar threw one of his ensnaring tentacles into the hole and pulled himself inside. He dangled at the opening for a moment, looking back across the ravine. Another glint of light—lower than the first—was moving, disappearing and reappearing every few seconds.

"Those have to be the ruins," he said. "And someone is exploring them." Well, at least one group wouldn't be rushing to these caves.

Time to find Cor and get out of here, Iltar thought, gently setting himself down in the small tunnel.

10

A WARRIOR'S FATE

"During the male's excavation, the female became ravenous. She would engorge herself on the newly formed crystal tunnel. The male would then create a larger opening. Eventually, the tunnel would be of sufficient size, and then the male would begin hollowing a den."

- From *History of the Eshari*, page 12

The tunnel Iltar had accidently carved was longer than he realized. At one point, he could not see either end. Only the light from his ensnaring spell illuminated the tight space.

Eventually, Iltar came to the opening that led to the curving cavern. He flinched upon seeing his reanimated minions. Every bone of each skeleton was transparent crystal. The skeletons glistened with pale-blue light mingled with the dark-purple hue of Iltar's reanimating magic.

The crysillac had used its power against the skeletons, but that change hadn't stopped the reanimated minions.

That's why the crysillac fled. The monster probably expected them to freeze mid-motion. *Must have scared the beast.* He chuckled.

Amid his mirth, Iltar eyed the distance between the hole and the cavern floor. It was too far to jump safely.

Still maintaining his ensnaring spell, Iltar shot one tentacle to the cavern's ceiling, then leapt from the opening. The magic slowed his fall, and he landed gently on the crystalline floor.

Iltar swiftly dismissed the dark-green tentacle, then searched for Cornar. His senses indicated that the warrior was still in the same area as before.

He must be trapped, Iltar thought, then dashed through the cavern.

Iltar passed several twists and turns until he felt Cornar to his right. He found a branching tunnel and dashed through it. But as Iltar ran, faint clicking noises echoed into the tunnel.

Oh no...

He halted, the crystallized skeletons assembling around him.

Iltar immediately drew upon the Darkness magic, forming a new necrotic sphere of protection. He was not running headlong into danger without a barsion.

Once the black barrier formed, Iltar continued toward Cornar. The magic enhancing the warrior was close. Very close. All the while, the clicking noises grew louder.

The cavern forked again, and Iltar took the left branch. He rounded the corner into a dead-end cave and jumped.

Three juvenile crysillacs—twice as long as a man was tall—scurried about the cavern floor, weaving around the skeletal remains of creatures native to the Abodine Wasteland. Each of the crysillacs was focused across the cavern, eyeing a narrow niche where Cornar stood with weapons drawn.

Cornar looked exhausted, his wavy brown hair disheveled and matted with sweat. He wore only his armor, and both his blades glowed a pale blue. Was that magic from the crysillac? The brown coat he had worn was nowhere to be seen. Blood dripped down Cornar's face from a gash across his cheek.

"Cor!" Iltar cried, then commanded his reanimated minions to attack the crysillacs.

The warrior spared Iltar a surprised glance, but returned his focus to the monsters eyeing him.

One of the crysillacs lunged toward Cornar, but he swung his weapons through the air and the monster backed away.

"Where's Dugan?" Cornar demanded, his tone fierce.

Iltar eyed two other juvenile crysillacs lying on the ground before answering. "I don't know," he said. "Probably dead."

"Heleron damn that monster," Cornar shouted. Amid his cursing, the leading skeletons reached the nearest crysillac and tackled it. Another crysillac scurried toward Cornar, and the warrior swung his weapons at it. The crysillac backed off, but several of Iltar's minions leapt upon the monster, pinning it to the ground.

The subdued crysillacs chirped, and the one who had initially attacked Cornar scurried across the cavern, attempting to evade the rest of Iltar's minions. Now freed, Cornar dashed toward Iltar, passing a pale-blue dome on the ground.

What is that—? Iltar's eyes widened with realization. The dome was Cornar's coat turned crystal. *Poor man must be freezing,* Iltar thought.

"I'm sure glad to see you," Cornar said, teeth chattering. "I didn't know how much longer I was going to last."

"What happened to your coat?" Iltar asked, dismissing his black barrier. He quickly removed his own coat as the warrior answered.

"They transmuted it." Cornar gestured to the limp crysillacs. "Once my barsion was gone I was struck by one of the tentacles. Fearful of your tale from earlier I threw it off. Luckily the crystallization of my coat didn't spread to me. I killed the ones with tentacles, but the others weren't as aggressive. Probably fearful of this." He shook his weapons. "My blades managed to trap the magic from the two I killed."

Iltar frowned, then extended his coat toward Cornar. "Here," he said, "take it."

"I'll be fine."

"No, you won't. Take it."

Cornar reluctantly took the coat. "You'll get cold, too."

"We'll take turns wearing it."

As the warrior donned the warm fur, Iltar uttered an incantation, mustering vibrant green particles—arpran magic.

The power of the Arpran Channel of Magic was purely restorative. With an arpran spell, a mage could heal wounds, cure disease, and prevent injury. Some mages and scholars believed arpran magic could regenerate lost limbs, but Iltar had never seen such a feat. Though arpran magic could heal, it could not reach beyond the veil of death.

Nothing could do that.

Vibrant green light burst from Iltar's hands, encircling Cornar. He couldn't tell if Cornar was already suffering the effects of frostbite. If he were, the arpran magic would heal him. Arpran magic wouldn't keep him warm, but it would reverse any damage caused by the cold and heal that gash.

"Thank you," Cornar said. He shivered once before explaining the ordeal of his fall and how he found himself in this den of young crysillacs. The monsters had attacked him immediately. Cornar supposed they thought he was food, judging by the carcasses in the cavern.

As the arpran magic healed Cornar, Iltar eyed the crysillacs struggling with the reanimated skeletons. None had tentacles protruding from their carapaces, but each had tiny bumps on their backs. *Females...* Iltar settled his gaze on the other two lying on the crystalline floor. Each had forearm-length pale-blue tentacles protruding from their carapaces. The tentacles were limp and did not glow.

"... maybe they're younger and not as violent," Cornar speculated. "Those three became wary after I killed the other two—"

"No, they're females," Iltar interrupted. "Only the males have tentacles. Females have spikes."

Cornar nodded, then wiped the blood from his cheek. The gash was gone. "Thank you," he said through a shiver, eyeing the skirmish between the creatures and skeletons. The cankered weapons did nothing to the crysillacs' carapaces and chitinous limbs.

"Do you know where we are?" Cornar asked.

"No clue." Iltar chuckled awkwardly. "But I think I

know of a way we can escape these nightmarish caverns."

"Oh?" Cornar's customary good humor returned. "Pray tell."

Iltar turned to Cornar and grinned. "We ascend the shaft that brought you here."

Cornar nodded. He glanced at his weapons, then swiftly hacked at the nearest carcass. The pale-blue light spread from the weapons and engulfed the bones, turning them to transparent crystal. Once the magic dissipated from the blades, Cornar sheathed his weapons.

"All right, let's go."

"The crysillacs were practical creatures, mating only when a den was hollowed."

\- From *History of the Eshari*, page 12

Iltar mustered his ensnaring tentacles as he followed Cornar across the cavern. Each of the young crysillacs was pinned by the skeletons, chirping incessantly.

"Here it is," Cornar said, pointing partway up the cavern wall. The opening was angled, and Iltar imagined Cornar must have slid most of the way. *Perhaps the friction of his fall dissipated his barsion.*

"Are you going to leave your skeletons?" Cornar asked.

"Yes," Iltar said. "These monsters are fairly intelligent. I don't want the young scurrying off to warn the big one, or wake the female."

"There's *another?*" Cornar asked warily.

Iltar nodded, then directed his spell in four directions. One vine-like tentacle wrapped around his waist, another grabbed Cornar, and a third sped toward the shaft followed by a fourth. Within seconds, they were ascending the shaft.

"And it was bigger," Iltar added. He propelled them through the shaft, just as he had climbed the ravine. "It was sleeping, though. And it looked pregnant."

"How could you tell that?" Cornar asked.

"Its belly was distended."

As they ascended the shaft, Iltar briefly related his ordeal after their separation. The tale intrigued Cornar, who was more than fond of peril. He reveled in it.

"Well, I don't imagine this thing will let us leave," Cornar said. "We trespassed on its territory and attacked it."

"Do you think it will chase us beyond the cave?" Iltar asked. After his last encounter with the monster, Iltar had hoped he could find Cornar and escape. The crysillac was *too* formidable.

"Yes," Cornar said. "Another clash is inevitable. And there is no telling how far it will chase us."

Iltar did not like the idea of fighting the crysillac again. The monster was too clever. But Cornar's argument was valid. To the crysillac they were pesky vermin. They were rats infesting its home.

But we can't fight it again in here, Iltar thought. Especially not while encased in any sort of destructive barsion. The crysillac would use the barsions to its advantage.

"We should draw it outside," Cornar said. "Fight it on the plains. If your estimations are correct, the others will be here soon. Unless they have already reached the tunnels and entered the caverns."

That would be disastrous. The others would start exploring in groups of three and the crysillac would pick them off one trio at a time.

"I hope they haven't arrived," Iltar said.

Cornar grunted. "We should escape invisibly," he said. "I know we don't have ropes to tie ourselves together, but perhaps you can weave one with your magic."

"That would work," Iltar nodded. Usually, if their band traveled invisibly they would break up into their groups of three, tie a rope around each other, and then the mages would cast their concealing magic.

"Do you really think Dugan is dead?" Cornar asked.

"I can't sense any of the magic I cast on him," Iltar said. "I see no way he could have survived."

Cornar sighed with disappointment.

They ascended the rest of the shaft in silence. Iltar thought about tactics they would use out on the plains. He would have to encase himself and Cornar in the Darkness magic. Barsions made from that power would be easier to maintain, as he would simply will more of the magic to reinforce their barriers. He saw no other way to successfully protect them from the crysillac's innate magic.

But then there was the matter of fatiguing himself. If he used the Darkness magic so extensively he would risk losing his focus—which would cause all his magic to dissipate. Only once had he succumbed to such strain and that nearly cost him and Cornar their lives. At the moment, Iltar felt no such strain, but... *No*, he thought, pushing aside the thought.

They soon arrived at the crysillac's lair. Iltar set both himself and Cornar on the cavern floor, then dismissed his magic.

Sharp pain pricked Iltar's arms. He rubbed his chest while taking in a deep breath.

"Are you cold?" Cornar asked.

"A little," Iltar said.

"Do you want your coat back?"

Iltar shook his head, then uttered an incantation, mustering more arpran magic. This spell, however, would persist within him. He'd have to cast another on Cornar. They could survive the deathly chill of the wasteland as long as he kept the arpran magic flowing within them. They would be cold, but the chilling affects would not be life-threatening.

Vibrant green light penetrated Iltar, surging across his entire body. The stinging pain dissipated. Though he was cold, it did not hurt. The chill was more uncomfortable and irritating than painful.

"I'll weave a cord, then conceal us," Iltar said. He cast another spell and pale-green fibers of light wove through the air. Cords woven from magic were nigh indestructible unless a dispel was cast upon them.

Once the cord formed, Iltar tossed one end to Cornar. As the warrior caught it, Iltar uttered the incantation to muster his veil of invisibility, and they both vanished.

"I assume you know the way out of here?" Iltar asked.

"Of course." Cornar chuckled. "We only traveled in a straight line. Even if we hadn't, you know I could find my way." Cornar's uncanny sense of direction was a well-known trait among their band of adventurers.

Iltar felt a tug against the rope, and he followed the invisible Cornar through the crysillac's lair. Cornar made an awe-filled remark about the hole that had swallowed Iltar, but continued toward the cavernous tunnel leading to the surface.

They left the creature's enormous lair, following the twists and turns of the large tunnel.

As they rounded one of the bends, both men started with horror.

Dugan stood before them, frozen in an expression of utter dread. The man had been turned to pale-blue crystal, along with his weapons and armor. Every bit of him was transparent, down to his bones and organs. Even his veins were visible beneath the surface of his crystallized skin.

"By Heleron's Trident!" Cornar cursed.

You poor fool, Iltar thought, gazing at the crystallized Dugan.

Cornar's invisible hand grabbed Dugan's sword-breaker, and he lifted it from the crystallized warrior.

He's not one solid hunk of crystal, Iltar thought, intrigued. *Like the bones of my minions.* He mused on the nature of the crysillac's power, but Cornar interrupted him by tugging on the magical rope.

"Let's get to the surface," Cornar murmured. The sight of one of his warriors slain in such a horrific way had enraged him.

12

PREPARATIONS

"After the male completed the den and the female was impregnated, the male would begin burrowing other tunnels. The process of creating additional tunnels took much longer, as the female would go into a state of hibernation during the first few years of her gestational cycle."

- From *History of the Eshari*, page 14

A freezing gust whipped through the crystallized tunnel. The biting chill stung Iltar briefly, but the pain dissipated soon after. They were close to the cave's entrance.

"We should set up on the snowdrift," Cornar said. He had remained silent since leaving the crystallized Dugan. Iltar hadn't spoken either. He didn't want to prematurely draw the attention of the crysillac.

"Once we're ready, you should make illusions of us," Cornar said. "Use them to draw the beast to us."

Iltar nodded, dismissing their invisibility.

They strode through the cave's mouth, moving straight

for the marker on the snowdrift.

"You can have your coat back," Cornar said. "I want to be completely encased in your Darkness magic, so I will be plenty warm. Besides, I'll be moving around enough that I will probably overheat if I keep wearing it."

"That's fine," Iltar said. "You will have an arpran regeneration maintaining you too."

Cornar nodded. "Can you pin the beast somehow?" the warrior asked. "If you can keep its claws away from me I can move about more easily."

"Yes," Iltar said. "I'll use some ensnaring tentacles. Hopefully that will hold. Otherwise, I can try to transmute something big. But that will take some time to create."

"Transmute whatever you're going to use before you send the illusions in," Cornar said. "I want to be fully prepared to kill this thing before we lure it out."

Cornar elaborated on his part while ascending the snowdrift. He intended to immobilize the monster by severing its legs. Once it was debilitated enough, Cornar would try to cut his way to the crysillac's brain. He hoped the brain was in its head, though they had encountered creatures that had brains in the oddest of places.

While Cornar was enacting his part of the plan Iltar would focus on destroying the tentacles, the monster's most lethal feature.

Once on the snowdrift, Cornar studied the surrounding area. "Let's lure it over there," the warrior said, pointing to a vast plain to their left. "There is a lot more space there than in front of the cave."

Cornar turned, looking at the markers they had set. "It looks like we're on our own. I would have preferred the reinforcements, but at least no one else will succumb to the horrors of that cave."

Iltar nodded gravely.

"No snide remark, my friend?" Cornar asked, chuckling. "Here I thought you would say you'd prefer it this way."

That lightened Iltar's mood, and he grinned at Cornar. "And you would ask if it was because it would be easier to protect only us."

Cornar laughed. "And your reply would be that you would not want the others in our way."

They both laughed. Cornar and Iltar had been like brothers for nearly thirty years. Perhaps if the current situation weren't so precarious, the conversation would have gone that way.

Cornar quelled his mirth and took off his borrowed coat. He handed it to its owner, and Iltar quickly wrapped himself in it, embracing the warmth.

With that, Iltar began mustering his magic, starting with the arpran regeneration. He then imbued Cornar's weapons with the Darkness magic. Both serrated dagger and short-sword glowed with black light. Cornar did not want any of the other magics imbuing his weapons. The Darkness was enough to accomplish the task ahead.

Once Cornar's weapons were imbued, Iltar encased the warrior in a form-fitting veil of the Darkness magic. Cornar practically vanished beneath the black mist. *You look like death itself,* Iltar mused.

"I'm going to get into position," Cornar said, crossing the snowdrift.

Iltar nodded, mustering his necrotic sphere of protection. He then uttered an incantation to create an illusion of himself. He figured one would be enough. The crysillac probably supposed Cornar was long dead. *Better to surprise the beast*, he thought.

As the illusion formed in front of him, Iltar sensed a jolt through his reanimated minions. He redirected his focus, concentrating on *seeing* through the magic that held the bones together.

Several of the skeletons were thrust from the young crysillac they were holding.

It couldn't be...

Through his magic, Iltar sensed the large crysillac. It attacked the reanimated minions, freeing its young.

"Cor!" Iltar shouted, interrupting the formation of his illusion. The illusory magic dissipated and wisped away.

Iltar put all his focus on one of the reanimated skeletons, sensing the scuffle. The young crysillacs had fled under the protection of the larger one, chirping loudly. The larger crysillac then replied, though the sounds coming from it were bellowing.

Were they speaking? Iltar wondered. The beast was intelligent; perhaps the monsters had a language of their own. If so, then—

The large crysillac turned from the dead-end cave and the young dispersed. The monster was no longer concerned with the reanimated minions.

Oh no, they told the big one about—

Iltar cut the thought short, forcing the skeleton into a run. The crysillac burst from the dead-end cave, pincers clicking. The skeleton dashed into the adjoining tunnel as the monster's tails whipped by.

Grab one! Iltar commanded, and the skeleton lunged,

gripping the very end of the crysillac's right tail.

"Cor, it's coming!" Iltar shouted.

The warrior spun to face the cave.

Through the magic reanimating the skeleton, Iltar sensed the crysillac speeding through the crystalline caverns.

Iltar clenched his teeth. "It's moving too fast." He wouldn't have time to transmute something large enough to pin the beast. "The ensnaring tentacles better be enough."

"Once a mated pair of crysillacs birthed offspring, the young helped excavate the caves until they matured. Young crysillacs often stayed in those caves for upwards of two hundred years before venturing out on their own."

- From *History of the Eshari*, page 17

Dark-green light swirled around Iltar's hands as he uttered the incantation to muster his ensnaring magic. As the magic coalesced, Iltar glimpsed Cornar dashing to the cave. The warrior left behind a trail of blackness that dissolved the snow.

Thick vine-like tentacles soon formed in a tight mass between Iltar's fingers. *Now the globes*, he told himself. Through his reanimated skeleton, Iltar sensed the crysillac nearing the cave's mouth. He glanced to Cornar, who skidded to a halt. The warrior dropped into a wide battle stance outside the cave entrance, weapons ready. With their plan ruined, Cornar probably wanted to intercept the beast at the cave and lure it to the plains.

We're going to have to fight it here, Iltar thought and closed his eyes, mustering more of the Darkness magic. Streams of black mist formed vague sphere-shapes that hovered around him. Nearly a dozen globes of darkness took shape, but Iltar continued streaming the black mist from his pores. Another ten orbs formed, and a burst of anger surged through him.

Not nearly enough, he thought as he closed his eyes to concentrate. More of the black orbs formed, but his anger intensified. *Control your rage*, he chided himself. His temper always intensified the more abundantly he used the Darkness magic. He had rarely used *this* much of the corrosive power.

As the globes of darkness formed, Iltar sensed the crysillac rounding the last bend.

"It's coming!" Iltar shouted, opening his eyes.

Faint clicking reached Iltar's ears, and then the crysillac burst from the cave, pale-blue tentacles flailing. Cornar lunged toward the beast, arms spread. The warrior leapt into the air, but the monster swatted at him with its corroded claw.

Cornar flew backward, but not before a black mist spread across the claw, dissolving more of the crustacean-like limb.

Amid anguished howling, the crysillac charged toward Iltar.

So much for our plan, Iltar grumbled, then unleashed his ensnaring spell.

The dark-green mass burst through the necrotic sphere of protection, and the vine-like tentacles flew wildly toward the crysillac, undulating in the freezing air.

Halfway between Iltar and the cave, the crysillac reared up, snapping its six claws. The beast bent its head toward Iltar, red eyes glaring in fury. A bellowing cry burst from the monster's octagonal mouth, causing its sharp opposable fangs to splay toward Iltar.

The crysillac dove as Iltar's ensnaring tentacles wrapped around it, binding its head and limbs while latching onto the snowy ground. The monster jolted as the ensnaring magic stopped its charge just short of Iltar, its fangs nearly touching the necrotic sphere of protection.

Iltar wasted no time and unleashed his globes of darkness, but the crysillac was just as swift.

Several pale-blue tentacles immediately lashed toward Iltar. Three were struck by Iltar's black orbs, but two swept across his deadly barrier. Crystals formed in Iltar's necrotic sphere of protection, but were soon consumed.

Oh, no you don't! Iltar growled, maneuvering his globes of darkness.

Three black orbs struck the assailing tentacles, and soon each of the pale-blue limbs fell to the snowdrift.

The crysillac howled, and Iltar felt the force of that scream against his barsion.

Impressive.

More tentacles lashed toward Iltar. He intercepted three of the pale-blue limbs with his deadly projectiles, but narrowly missed the others. The beast was fast. The tentacles swept overhead, transforming the magic.

Crystals formed in the necrotic sphere of protection once again, but they were soon consumed.

Iltar redirected his globes of darkness, striking the sweeping tentacles. The Darkness magic spread through the pale-blue limbs, eroding the strange flesh.

The crysillac howled again, then jerked.

Was it struggling to break free—?

A flash of movement sped from Iltar's right and he started. The crysillac's tail swung toward him. *No!*

The monster's twin tail struck the snowdrift at an angle and then lifted the mound of snow into the air.

Iltar staggered, then completely lost his footing. The world turned sideways, and he felt himself racing through the air with the snowdrift *flying* beside him. He redirected his remaining globes of darkness, raining them down upon the monster.

Howls from the crysillac echoed across the wasteland as Iltar crashed into the snowy plain, burrowing through the snow. The snowdrift followed, sealing the hole formed by his necrotic sphere of protection.

Not again, Iltar groaned, dismissing his corrosive barsion. He fell against something cold and hard. With the snow-drift blocking the opening, the newly formed tunnel was dark. Iltar staggered to his feet and a sharp pain shot through his side. He gasped and another spike of pain surged through him. Most likely a broken rib.

The pain soon subsided as his arpran regeneration healed him. That spell, however, faded.

"That beast really *is* intelligent," he grumbled, edging through the darkness.

The tunnel was fairly shallow, and Iltar reformed his corrosive barrier as he climbed. As the necrotic sphere formed he felt a twinge of fatigue. *No!* he chided himself. Taking a renewing breath, Iltar reached out to his reani-mated minion, who was hurled another direction. The force of the tail striking the snowdrift had sent the skeleton flying.

Attack, Iltar commanded, and the reanimated skeleton dashed across the frozen plain.

Soon, Iltar reached the snowdrift blocking the opening, and his necrotic sphere of protection eroded the packed snow swifter than a burning fire.

He stumbled outside, finding himself near the plain where they had intended to lure the crysillac.

"Ironic," he muttered, studying the battle between Cornar and the monster.

Cornar swiftly assailed the crysillac, weaving between the monster's legs. He evaded pincers and tentacles as he sliced at the chitinous legs, severing limb after limb. When Cornar fought he was a wonder to behold.

In an attempt to retaliate, the monster swung its tails toward Cornar.

The warrior threw himself sideways, rolling across the ground. Cornar disappeared from view, but soon rebounded onto his feet. He moved to the nearest leg and sliced through it.

His barsion is holding, Iltar thought, sensing the barrier's integrity. The observation came as a relief.

Cornar evaded another swipe from the crysillac's tails.

Those tails—and the rear legs—needed to be disabled.

Iltar immediately uttered another incantation, mustering more of his ensnaring magic. As the vine-like strands formed, Iltar felt his initial ensnaring spell weakening.

How was that possible?

Still focused on the incantation, Iltar glanced at the magic binding the monster.

The crysillac was using its innate magical abilities on the ensnaring tentacles. One of the vine-like tendrils binding the creature was partly blue. Others had pale-blue spots that were spreading.

Iltar finished the incantation and hurled the ensnaring magic through the air. The dark-green mass erupted behind the monster, the forming vine-like tentacles flailing wildly. The ensnaring tentacles gripped the crysillac's tails and many of its legs while latching to the snowy ground.

I'll need to muster more, Iltar thought. But managing each of those ensnaring spells would be taxing...

As he opened his mouth to utter another incantation, a shadow passed over him. "What now?" he said, grumbling and glancing skyward.

"*A female crysillac could give birth to upward of ten infants at a time. At the height of a pair's parenthood, a hundred crysillacs could occupy a den.*"

- From *History of the Eshari*, page 18

A white bird circled above Iltar. It turned, revealing its long neck. A pale-yellow patch covered the crown of its head, and black tips marked the edges of its wings.

A gosset? Iltar narrowed his eyes in thought. Gossets never flew this far south. That could mean only one thing.

Iltar spun and stared across the snowy plain, searching for the rest of his adventuring band. But there was no sight of them.

A squawk drew his attention, and he turned to see the gosset plummeting into the snow. Gossets often dove into the water to catch their prey. *I suppose snow isn't much different*, Iltar thought. The bird disappeared for a moment, then waddled out of the tunnel it had carved.

"Amendal, is that you?" Iltar asked the bird.

The gosset nodded and then pointed a wing across the plain. Amendal—the crazed conjurer—*was* controlling the bird. This gosset was a conjuration, a duplicate of an actual gosset Amendal had lured through a portal long ago. Now, he was able to manifest replicas of the bird through his conjuration magic.

Suddenly, the conjured gosset stamped a pattern in the snow. The prints formed letters and then words.

"*Are you okay?*"

"Not really," Iltar said, and sighed. "Dugan is dead, and we're fighting a crysillac."

The bird started, then abruptly spun as if searching for something. Had Amendal not seen Cornar and the crysillac?

Frantic squawking left the conjuration's beak as the bird saw the battle. The gosset jumped repeatedly and flapped its wings.

Amendal was definitely controlling the bird.

"Hurry," Iltar said, returning his focus to the battle. He walked from the conjured bird, but not too far. He wanted to keep his distance from the battle. Iltar would assail the crysillac from afar.

He uttered an incantation, mustering another ensnaring spell, and flung the dark-green mass, reinforcing the first set of ensnaring tentacles. He then mustered more of the Darkness magic. Both magics taxed his focus, and he fought back a wave of tiredness. All the while, the conjuration continued squawking.

"I can't understand you, Amendal," Iltar sighed, exasperated. Amendal had a tendency to try to talk *through* his conjurations. It worked fine for certain animals, creatures with complex vocal cords, but not gossets.

Ignoring the conjurer, Iltar streamed more of the Darkness magic from his pores. The act taxed him further while stoking his anger. Two dozen globes of darkness formed around Iltar, and he hurled them across the frozen plain. He guided each toward one of the many pale-blue tentacles swatting at Cornar. Several struck the monster, but Iltar missed nearly half the time. His bad aim was partly due to his fatigue and the crysillac's nimbleness.

Despite all the tentacles Iltar had severed, the crysillac still had plenty. There had to be over a hundred of them.

Cornar's efforts looked equally futile. The warrior had severed maybe a tenth of the chitinous legs.

Perhaps it is good that the others are near, Iltar thought, forming more of his globes of darkness. It would take an army to slay the monster.

As Iltar flung the deadly orbs, the conjured gosset waddled up beside him. The bird squawked once, then waddled in front of Iltar. It cocked its head, as if demanding an answer.

"What do you want, Amendal?" Iltar asked dismissively, focused on mustering more of his deadly magic.

The bird stamped in the snow, forming more words.

Iltar ignored the conjuration. His reanimated skeleton was nearing the battle. Though it lacked any weapons, Iltar could still use it as a distraction.

An angry squawk left the bird's beak, and Iltar glanced to the crude words in the snow.

"Stop attacking! Don't kill it!"

"Why?" Iltar asked. "You won't be able to suck it

through a portal. All the myths say they are impervious to enthralling effects. There is no way for you to add this beast to your menagerie of monsters."

The bird gave him a perturbed glance.

Iltar sighed. "Besides, you're telling the wrong person, Amendal. I'm just trying to disable it. Cornar is the one you should be talking to."

The conjuration flung a wing toward the battle, squawking incessantly.

You irritating old man... Iltar thought. Perhaps old was not the right word to describe Amendal. He was only in his mid-sixties, but he was twenty-five years Iltar's senior. *Old enough*, he groused.

With that, Iltar mustered more of the Darkness magic. Amendal was delusional if he thought he could draw the crysillac into a conjuration portal. If Iltar thought an enthralling spell would work on the crysillac, he would have coerced the monster within its lair.

Amendal could try all he wanted when he arrived, but Iltar would not cease his assault. Besides, the crysillac was holding its own. The party would probably reach the battle long before the beast was disabled, let alone killed.

15

HUBRIS

"Crysillacs repeated the cycle of creating dens and mating for their entire lives, leaving behind quite a legacy of warrens and caverns. One particular group of Eshari discovered a network of crysillac caves that spread farther than the grandest cities of Kalda."

- From *History of the Eshari*, page 21

Iltar no longer felt his ensnaring tentacles gripping the crysillac's left claws. He shifted his focus, eyeing the green magic turned pale-blue crystal. Iltar could scarcely believe the sight.

The crysillac struggled against the crystal bindings, causing them to crack. *Oh no...* In any other circumstance Iltar would have thought the beast impressive.

Fighting against the fatigue, Iltar flung another globe of darkness as a roaring crackle rumbled above him. *Lightning?*

Thick clouds gathered over the battlefield, lightning surging through them. The clouds had unnaturally appeared out of nowhere.

The gosset squawked, then fluttered away.

They're here, Iltar thought, glancing across the frozen plain.

Dashing figures crested a distant snowdrift, running at incredible speed. Each was surrounded by brightly colored barsion barriers and wielded weapons gleaming with various destructive magics.

Thunder clapped above Iltar, and he glanced to the unnatural clouds. The storm resulted from a combined spell from several elementalists. There were three in Iltar's band: Hex, Baekal, and Shurin.

Golden light formed across the plain—a conjuration portal. The golden magic spread, forming an oval shape five times the height of a man. Soon, a humanoid shape appeared within the golden light, nearly filling the portal. An enormous earthen hand stretched from the mystical doorway, followed by an equally massive foot. More limbs emerged, then a colossal behemoth of living rock and dirt stepped onto the frozen plain. The earthen gargantuan bounded past the dashing figures, moving straight for the crysillac.

More figures crested the distant snowdrift, each surrounded by brightly colored bubbles of barsion—the other mages of Iltar's band. The light of various destructive spells coalesced around each of them.

It doesn't look like anyone else is listening to Amendal, Iltar thought, mustering more of his deadly projectiles. The forming magic taxed him further, but he couldn't give into fatigue—not now.

A resounding crash echoed from the battle, and Iltar

turned to see the earthen gargantuan atop the crysillac. The conjuration slammed its rocky fists into the monster's golden carapace. Soon, the dashing figures—the party's warriors—joined Cornar. All of them hacked at the crysillac's chitinous legs.

The monster attempted to retaliate, but the earthen giant took the brunt of the blows. Parts of the earthen conjuration were turning a transparent pale blue. But despite the change, the earthen giant continued attacking.

A crack echoed from the battlefield, and parts of the monster's carapace fell in pieces around the warriors.

Iltar flung each of his orbs, severing more tentacles. With the reinforcements the crysillac was too distracted to effectively evade Iltar's magic.

With the party gathered, the battle intensified.

Cornar and his warriors hacked at the monster's limbs. Thunder resounded, then a blinding flash shot from the dark clouds. Dozens of lightning bolts struck the crysillac, surging across it. The monster shrieked, but continued thrashing. The mages unleashed their destructive magics, striking the monster's tentacles—several erupted into flame while violet orbs disintegrated others.

Despite all their efforts, the crysillac still had many of its limbs. Not to mention, the monster showed no signs of relenting.

"This is taking too long," Iltar muttered, furrowing his brow.

An idea soon came to him, one he had not considered.

If I strike the beast with a blast of the Darkness magic, perhaps I can end this. It would take a considerable amount of time to muster that much of the corrosive power, and he would need to be closer. The idea was dangerous, since mustering that much of the Darkness magic might exhaust him to the point of collapse. That would leave both him and Cornar vulnerable. But if it worked, then the battle would be over.

Iltar splayed his hands and strode toward the battle, straining against the advancing fatigue of mustering the Darkness magic.

While Iltar advanced, another of his band dashed to the battle with arms flailing. The newcomer was shouting, what exactly Iltar couldn't tell. As he converged with the newcomer, Iltar recognized the frantic man.

It was Amendal.

"Stop, you idiots!" the crazed conjurer shouted. "You'll kill it!"

A beam of violet light shot from the distant snowdrift, striking the right shoulder of the crysillac's middle claw. The beam instantly disintegrated the joint, and the claw— still bound by Iltar's magic—fell away from the monster.

"No, no, no!" Amendal shouted.

Iltar shook his head, black mists streaming around him. His anger was boiling, and some of his fatigue dissipated.

Another crack filled the air, and more of the carapace fell.

"Will you idiots stop for one moment?!" Amendal screamed.

Another flash of lightning shot from the dark clouds, electrifying the crysillac.

"Hex!" Amendal screamed, glancing back to the snowdrift. "No more lightning!" The crazed conjurer continued shouting to the others, but no one listened.

"It's futile, Amendal," Iltar shouted, nearly scowling. He had mustered so much of the Darkness magic that his anger had peaked. "The crysillac won't survive our onslaught!" He turned back to the battle, arms spread wide.

Amendal screamed incoherent babbling. Iltar had heard the gibberish before. The crazed conjurer claimed they were curses of a long-forgotten language. After his short tirade, Amendal uttered an incantation. Despite Iltar's warning, the crazed fool was going to try to trap the crysillac.

Idiot!

Iltar focused his eyes on the monster. His anger was raging now. He would kill that beast and mount its carcass!

Black streams nearly blocked Iltar's vision, and he focused on condensing them. The mists swirled to a singular point in front of him, gathering like a funnel.

Iltar felt himself reaching his mental capacity. He staggered against exhaustion. His necrotic sphere of protection flickered, then shattered. Parts of the black barsion wisped into the funnel.

"Now..." Iltar muttered, his hands shaking, "you... die..." More of the black mist seethed from his pores, and his arms trembled. Soon, his entire body shook in exhaustion.

Amendal finished his incantation, and charcoal light shot past Iltar, beaming toward the crysillac. That charcoal beam was the enthralling component used to draw creatures into a conjurer's portal.

Iltar's focus waned and he felt his other spells dissipating. One of the ensnaring tentacles flickered, then slithered away from the crysillac. The reanimating magic vanished, and the crystallized skeleton collapsed. Cornar's barsion weakened, but the black mists around his weapons persisted.

"Don't... die... Cor..."

More of the ensnaring tentacles dispersed, and the crysillac jolted, partially freed. Iltar felt the funnel of blackness brimming. His vision tunneled, and he became lightheaded.

"Now... or never—"

Amendal's enthralling magic struck the crysillac, and the monster stilled abruptly.

A triumphant cackle resounded behind Iltar. "I did it!" Amendal shouted, sounding deranged. "The myths were wrong!" he cackled, then continued ranting. "It's mine! All mine!"

Did Iltar dare unleash the blast? Was the monster really under the crazed fool's control?

The rest of the ensnaring tentacles dissipated, and those parts that had been crystallized fell. They kicked up snow, dousing the warriors. The crysillac, however, remained still.

A faint voice murmured in the back of Iltar's head, but he couldn't make out what it was saying. It sounded as if it were repeating a single word... The shift in focus disrupted his control, and the funnel of blackness weakened. But Iltar felt no less strained.

Amid his quandary, the earthen gargantuan backed away from the crysillac. Much of the conjured creature had been crystallized, and it struggled to move. Its footsteps shook the ground, and Iltar suddenly felt dizzy, his vision blurring.

"Yes! Come to me, you ancient wonder," Amendal cried. "Join my menagerie! You will revel with the others, especially the gangolins."

Iltar furrowed his brow as the crysillac lumbered toward him while the warriors backed away from the beast. Had the old fool actually enthralled it? There was no other reason for the warriors to cease their assault.

That voice in Iltar's mind was even fainter than before, more an irritating buzz. He glanced to Amendal, who stood beside an enormous golden portal the size of the cave.

Amendal had succeeded.

Iltar quickly dismissed the Darkness magic. The funnel of blackness vanished, as did his anger. He sucked in his breath, regaining his composure but collapsing to the ground, his strength spent.

Under Amendal's control, the crysillac lumbered toward the gateway to another plane of reality, a place where time did not exist, a place that conjurers called the Visirm Expanse.

Iltar eyed the lumbering crysillac, confused. *So, the myths were wrong…* After all, myths weren't entirely accurate. The tale of the crysillac claimed that no one could control the beast.

But Amendal was controlling it. The crysillac stepped into the conjuration portal, then was sucked into the golden light, vanishing completely.

16

CESSATION

"After centuries of study, a group of Eshari managed to lure a mated pair of crysillacs to a mountainous spot near the city of Vabinodol. The Eshari used crystals harvested from abandoned caves as offerings."

- From *History of the Eshari*, page 41

The rumble of thunder faded overhead, and the dark storm clouds dispersed.

Still kneeling in the snow, Iltar scanned the snow-covered valley as the rest of his adventuring band approached. Cornar jogged with many of his warriors while the mages descended the snowdrift.

Amendal whooped triumphantly as his conjuration portal collapsed, trapping the crysillac. The monster would forever remain alive, untouched by time in a form of stasis. From that point on, Amendal could conjure a crysillac—well, a duplicate of a maimed one.

"I did it!" Amendal shouted. The conjurer danced in the snow, throwing his hands into the air. "The crysillac is mine! Now I can turn anyone who crosses me into crystal!" He cackled with diabolical glee.

Iltar raised his brow and pursed his lips, studying the crazed conjurer. "I'm impressed," he said, rising from the snow. "You accomplished the impossible."

"Of course I did!" Amendal clapped his hands. "There is not a greater conjurer than I!" He cocked his head, gazing skyward, a childish grin spreading across his face.

You really are crazy, Amendal, Iltar thought.

"I thought that thing couldn't be enthralled," Cornar shouted. The black barrier around him was barely visible.

"It seems the myth was inaccurate," Iltar said. He dismissed the warrior's barsion, and it wisped away.

"Of course it was," Amendal declared. "Someone obviously created that erroneous idea to dissuade anyone from seeking the creatures." The crazed conjurer continued his speculation, delivering a discourse that implied his words were fact. Amendal assumed that the originator of the myth was trying to protect the crysillacs. Their numbers had dwindled during the fabled Dragon Wars, and they were in danger of extinction.

Iltar was not convinced. Especially upon hearing Amendal mention the Dragon Wars. *What nonsense*, he thought. The Dragon Wars were not real. *Tales made up to inspire men. That's all they are.*

"Well, I wish *you* had tried enthralling it," Cornar said to Iltar.

Iltar was not amused. "And if I had failed? Then what?"

"Well, we were already fighting the beast," Cornar replied.

The other mages arrived soon after, lanky Hex in the

lead.

"I'm glad you're safe!" Hex exclaimed, running a hand through his wavy blond hair. "When you didn't return, we feared something happened to you."

Cornar smiled, nodding at Hex. "Where are the others?" he asked.

Iltar looked about. Several trios were missing.

"They went after Hagen's group," Hex replied. "When we left, his group hadn't returned either."

Cornar gave Iltar a knowing glance. Hagen's group had probably been the ones Iltar noticed while in the ravine.

"Well, let's get back to camp," Cornar said. "Hopefully the others will be there when we return."

With the crysillac vanquished, the mages dismissed their magic, all except Hex. The wizard created a dome of fiery barsion above Cornar while Iltar infused the warrior with more arpran magic.

Once warmed, Cornar led everyone across the snowy plain. Many of the warriors asked questions about the ordeal within the caves, particularly concerning Dugan's demise. The answer horrified each of them.

They did not get far before faint clicking reached Iltar's ears.

No… he groaned, and spun, turning back to the cave. *Had the female awakened?*

Several others turned warily, and a few warriors—including Cornar—drew their weapons. The others, however, muttered confused questions. They had not heard the scurrying scrapes of the crysillac, and so they did not recognize the sound.

Iltar focused on the tunnel, and the clicking grew louder. Soon, the cave mouth darkened and the other crysillac appeared. The beast slowed and stopped at the cave's mouth. The crysillac's red eyes stared at the severed limbs of its mate, then glanced at the party, studying them.

"You didn't mention there was another one!" Amendal exclaimed. The crazed fool stepped ahead of the party and giddily approached the cave.

"Is that the female?" Cornar asked warily.

"I can't tell," Iltar said. This crysillac was so big it barely fit in the cave.

"Uh, Amendal..." Hex muttered. "What are you doing?"

"Fetching another one, of course," Amendal replied. "Why have one crysillac when you can have two?"

Cornar shook his head, as did many of the other warriors.

"Get back here," Iltar told the conjurer, but Amendal ignored him. All the while, the crysillac looked back and forth from the party to the severed remains of its mate.

"Amendal," Iltar yelled. *You better not provoke it*, he thought. But if this female was like those who had attacked Cornar, then perhaps it wouldn't be as hostile.

The crazed conjurer began uttering an incantation as he approached the cave, golden light gathering around him.

The crysillac studied Amendal, then slunk back into the cave. The clicking of its pincers soon faded.

Amendal dismissed his spell, then spun to the rest of the party. "We have to go after it!"

"No, Amendal!" Iltar and Cornar shouted in unison.

The crazed conjurer pursed his lips, then stalked back across the snow. "Now I'll only be able to conjure a gimped crysillac," Amendal grumbled, stomping past the party. "One with only half its legs, a third of its tentacles, and missing two of its claws. Not to mention, most of its eyes." Despite his old age, Amendal could be childish. He did have a point, though. Whenever he conjured a crysillac it would lack many of its limbs.

Iltar shook his head before glancing back to the cave. All was silent.

"That was close," Cornar sighed. "Now let's get back to camp."

17

FULL CIRCLE

"Something miraculous occurred after those offerings, begin-
ning a relationship between Eshari and crysillac that would
shape the Esharian Collective forever."

- From *History of the Eshari*, page 42

The sun had dipped to the horizon when Iltar and
his band reached their camp. To Iltar's surprise,
Hagen and his group were waiting for them, as
well as the other trios. Old Cedath was among those waiting, sitting by a fire with his great-nephew, Tilthan.

"Welcome back," Cedath said, rising from the fire. He
smoothed his long gray mustaches and studied Iltar and
Cornar. "Now what did you find that required you to stay
away all day?"

"The greatest prize of all!" Amendal chimed, raising a
fist triumphantly into the air. Then his expression soured.
"Well, part of it."

Iltar gave Amendal an annoyed glance while Cornar replied.

"A monster," the warrior said. "Well, several. And a labyrinth of crystal caverns."

"Really?" Cedath's eyes widened, intrigued. "Monsters? Out here in this god-forsaken place?"

"Yes," Iltar said. "I suppose you found the ruins?" He glanced to young Tilthan, who like his great-uncle was a thief. He had been trained by Cedath several years before and had joined Iltar's party. He was an irritating git. If it weren't for Cedath, Tilthan wouldn't be a part of Iltar's adventuring band.

"We sure did," Tilthan smiled smugly. "And brought back *everything*."

Cedath shook his head. "There wasn't much. Only three sacks full," the old thief said.

"Yeah," Tilthan said with a grunt. "I tried to convince Old Cedath here to let me have all the loot, since I'm the one who found it," he said sardonically. "Sure, Nordal and Hagen were with me, but I'm the one who spotted the ruins and found the hidden stashes. I practically did all the work myself."

Cornar swore under his breath, not amused by Tilthan's arrogance.

"What?" Tilthan shrugged innocently. "It's the truth."

Cedath ignored his great-nephew and looked to Iltar. "Do you want to divide the loot here or on Kenard's ship?"

"On the *White Duchess*," Iltar said.

Cedath nodded, then returned to the fire. The rest of the band who had reinforced Iltar and Cornar plodded through the camp, going back to their tents.

Soon, only Iltar, Cornar, and Hex remained in the cold.

"I don't suppose you want to see those ruins?" Cornar asked.

Iltar shook his head. "Not if they plundered it," he said. "We can start heading back after we rest."

"Good," Cornar said, then tromped off through the camp. "I'm cold and starving."

With that, both warrior and wizard wove between the tents, and Hex dismissed his magic warming Cornar. The warrior disappeared within a tent, then soon emerged with another thick brown coat.

Iltar, however, returned to the camp's edge. He stared back across the frozen plain. "Good riddance," Iltar murmured. Soon they would be back on Captain Kenard's ship and sailing home for Soroth.

"What an adventure," he whispered, reflecting on the perils of the day. While recalling the battle his thoughts lingered on the strange voice he had heard. Never had he heard a voice while mustering the Darkness magic. It had been like a faint cry carried on the wind, audible but not recognizable.

Was my mind playing tricks on me? Iltar wondered. *And what about that raging anger?*

He admitted that he had a temper, although he did his best to control it. Using the Darkness magic always evoked some measure of anger. But what he felt during the final moments of the battle was far greater than any fury he had ever experienced, and Iltar found the intensity worrisome.

Another drawback to that magic. Perhaps on his next adventure he would use the Darkness magic sparingly. A displeased murmur rumbled in the back of Iltar's mind as a strong gust blew across the plain. Iltar shuddered as a faint voice replaced the murmur, DO NOT FORSAKE YOUR DESTINY.

Iltar set his jaw. No, that voice could not have been real. *Just fatigue*, he thought. After all, the events of the day had been arduous. With that, Iltar returned to his tent, ready more than ever to leave this god-forsaken wasteland.

THE END OF

BENEATH THE FROZEN WASTES

GLOSSARY

A glossary of names, people, places, objects, and terms found in *Beneath the Frozen Wastes*. Pronunciations and brief descriptions or definitions included.

<u>Pronunciation Key:</u>

ə .... banana, collide, abut

ər.... further, merger, bird

a .... mat, map, mad, gag, snap, patch

ā .... day, fade, date, aorta, drape, cape

ä .... bother, cot

är .... car, heart, bazaar, bizarre

aů .... now, loud, out

e .... bet, bed, peck

er .... bare, fair, wear, millionaire

ē .... easy, mealy

i .... tip, banish, active

ir .... near, deer, mere, pier

ī .... site, side, buy, tripe

j .... job, gem, edge, join, judge

k .... kin, cook, ache

ḵ ....German ich, Buch;

loch

ŋ .... sing\'siŋ\, singer\siŋ-ər\, finger\'fiŋ-gər\, ink\iŋk

ō .... bone, know, beau

ȯ .... saw, all, gnaw, caught

ȯi .... coin, destroy

ȯr .... boar, port, door, shore

th .... thin, ether

<u>th</u> .... then, either, this

ü .... rule, youth, union, few

ů .... pull, wood, boo

ůr .... boor, tour, insure

zh .... vision, azure\'a-zher

' .... marks preceding syllable with primary stress

- .... marks syllable division

Abodal (ab'-ō-dal): elvish name for the Abodine Wasteland.

Abodine Wasteland (ab'-ō–dīn): the name for southernmost continent of Kalda, located on the planet's southern pole.

Amendal Aramien (ōmen'-dal | 'ə-rā-mē-en)*:* an old conjurer from Soroth well-known for his magical prowess and deranged mental state.

Arpran Magic (är-prən')*:* a type, or channel, or magic that can heal, regenerate, and prolong life.

Baekal (bāe-cal)*:* a female elementalist (wizardry sub-discipline), and Igan's wife.

Barsion (bär'-zhən)*:* a type, or channel, of protective magic used primarily to create defensive barriers, but it can also restrain.

Cedath (cē'-dəth)*:* an expert thief who possesses several unique tevisrals, and a member of Iltar and Cornar's adventuring band.

Channels of Magic: the system by which magic is categorized on the world of Kalda. It consists of seven distinct channels, or types of magic: arcane, arpran, barsion, conjuration, elemental, manipulation, transmutation.

Cisthyrn (cis-t͟hûrn')*:* wolf-like creatures that inhabit the Abodine Wasteland. Cisthyrn are twice the size of the average world, with pale-blue crystalline horns and claws. The whites of their eyes are blue while their irises are white.

Conjurer: a mage who accesses the Conjuration Channel of magic to access the Aldinal Plane and the Visirm Expanse. The Aldinal Plane contains raw matter while the Visirm Expanse is a timeless void

Cornar Dol'shir (kòr-när | dōl-shir)*:* a hearty warrior and co-leader of a band of adventurers.

Crysillac (cry'-sil-lak)*:* a subterranean behemoth attributed with the ability to turn anything it touches to crystal. They have dozens of legs and tentacles.

Darkness Magic: a black magic that devourers all it touches, sometimes leaving behind gray dust.

Dragon Wars: a mythical war rumored to have occurred thousands of years ago, waged between the factions of dragonkind.

Dugan (dŭ-gan): a warrior in Iltar and Cornar's band.

Elemental Channel: the channel of magic capable of manifesting naturally occurring forces, including: wind, water, fire, earth, ice, acid, magma, etc.

Elementalist: a subclass within the wizardly discipline, specializing in manifesting the Elemental Channel of magic.

Eshari (ē'-shär-ī): an ancient humanoid race who inhabited the Abodine Wasteland capable of thriving in the extreme cold. Their features resemble the elves of Kalda, but their skin is a pale-blue.

Gangolin (gāŋ-gȯl-in'): a mythical creature akin to a dragon, but without wings. Rumored extinct, but some claim gangolins roam the Melar Forest.

Globe of Darkness: a condensed palm-sized sphere of the "Darkness Magic" used by Iltar.

Gosset (gäs-set'): a white long-necked bird. Black tips mark the edges of the wings. Pale yellow feathers cover their crowns and run partway down their necks. When hunting for food they dive into the water.

Grand Mage: a magic wielder who specializes in accessing each of the seven Channels of Magic.

Heleron's Trident (hel-ǝr'-ȯn): a cursed some Kaldeans swear.

Hex: one of Iltar's trusted friends and an Elementalist.

*Igan (*í-gän*):* one of Iltar's trusted allies and an Arcanist, a wizard who specializes in the Arcane Discipline. Husband to Baekal.

Illusionist: a mage who specializes in the Manipulation Channel of magic, creating illusions, enhancements, and manipulations of the mind.

*Iltar (*íl-tär*):* a powerful mage from Soroth, and the co-leader of a band of adventurers. In addition to his prowess in accessing many of the Channels of Magic, he has an ability to manifest a power that devours all it touches—the Darkness Magic.

*Irum'mak'sha (*ír-üm-'mäk-shò*):* draconic title for the twelve dragons holding the highest knowledge for each Channel of Magic, or Channel of Power.

*Kaelyrn (*kā-lē-ůrn'*):* one of Kalda's moons which shines with speckled light.

*Kalda (*kòl-də'*):* the name of the World.

*Kardorth (*kär'-dòrth*):* one of the oldest elven cities and capitol of the elven realm.

*Kenard, Joselin (*ken'-ärd*):* a sea captain hired by Iltar and Cornar to ferry their adventuring band across the world. His ship, the *White Duchess* is one of the fastest vessels in all the world.

*Kistern (*kis-tůrn'*):* one of Kalda's moons who shines the brightest.

Lightstone: a stone capable of emitting magic in the form light. Lightstones are considered magical in nature. Some believe their light a result of tevisrals—magical objects—while others believe they are tevisrals.

Mage: any person who is trained to access the Channels

of Magic.

Necromancer: a mage class specializing in the darker arts of the various Channels of Magic. They are capable of reanimating the dead, siphoning the life of the living, and mustering corrosive magics.

Necrotic Sphere of Protection: a barsion-like manifest of the "Darkness Magic" that creates a devouring bubble around the wielder.

*Nordal (*nòr-dal'*):* a warrior trained by Cornar, and a member of Iltar's adventuring band. Originally from the city of Klath in the Kingdom of Los.

*Shurin (*shûr'-in*):* an elementalist and member of Iltar and Cornar's adventuring band.

*Soroth (*sòr'-òth*):* the capitol city of the island and nation sharing that same name. One of the larger ports in the Kalishir Ocean.

*Tardalim (*tär-dò-lim*):* the eternal prison of damned souls, the Hell of Kalda.

*Tevisral (*tev'-is-rəl*):* any device capable of manifesting or channeling magic.

Thousand Years War, the: a series of conflicts spanning over a millennium. It began when Cheserith, a red dragon, rebelled against his fellow Ril'Sha, seeking to lay claim to his right to rule all Kalda. It brought about a permanent schism between dragonkind. Among men it is commonly known as the "Dragon Wars" and is generally believed to be myth.

*Tilthan (*til-thän*):* the grand-nephew of Cedath and a thief from Klath who possesses a set of thieving tevisrals: a cloak capable of instantly veiling its wearer, lenses capable of detecting all sorts of magic, and a shape-shift rod.

Transmutative Magic: a type, or Channel, of magic that changes the composition of physical matter from one state to another.

Vabinodol *(vä'-bin-ȯ-dal):* an ancient Eshari city.

Vaerym *(vā-rim'):* a ferocious breed of amphibious horned serpents. Vaeryms are large creatures, sometimes growing as long as eighty phineals. They often kept below ice sheets, only breaking through if a creature dares traverse the frozen surface. Their bodies are covered in dark blue scales while their heads are shielded by black shells ending in a glistening black beak.

Visirm Expanse *(vis-ər'-m):* another plane of reality, a timeless void used by conjurers to trap creatures and objects they wish to summon at a future time.

White Duchess: Captain Kenard's sea vessel, made of a material that cannot rot nor rust. It has six decks, two above the main deck, and three masts.

Yaeltis *(yel'-tis):* burly creatures native to the colder parts of Kalda. They are cousins to trolls, but have thick white coats of fur. They also possess curved tusks that jut out from their lower jaws that are covered in lethal venom.

CONNECT WITH THE AUTHORS

Stay up to date on future releases, upcoming Kickstarter campaigns, booksignings, and author appearances by signing up for Dan Zangari & Robert Zangari's mailing list at:

http://www.legendsofkalda.com/newsletter.html

Official Facebook Page:
https://www.facebook.com/legendsofkalda

AUTHOR'S AFTERWORD

ROBERT ZANGARI

Originally, *Beneath the Frozen Wastes* was meant to be a monster-based short story that we intended to submit to anthology, but it turned out to be much larger than we expected. So, we decided to offer it as a free bonus to anyone who signed up on our mailing list.

We have plans to potentially expand the story into full length novel (80,000 to 100,000 words), along with several other adventures in Iltar and Cornar's past. But that will have to wait until we are finished with Tales of the Amulet.

Beneath the Frozen Wastes actually helped pave the groundwork for the prequel novel, *The Prisoner of Tardalim*, which we began writing after finishing this story.

All in all, this was a fun piece and we thoroughly enjoyed writing it. We hope you enjoyed it.

–Robert Zangari
Salt Lake City, 2019

ABOUT THE AUTHORS

Dan Zangari is the creator of the Legends of Kalda fantasy universe, a work-in-development since the early 1990's. He received a Bachelor's of Science in Aerospace Engineering from the University of Southern California and a Masters Degree in Systems Management. His love for science fiction and fantasy prompted the creation of this fantasy universe. When he's not writing he enjoys reading, watching movies, spending quality time with family and serving in his local church congregation.

Robert Zangari is the co-author of the various books which belong to the Legends of Kalda universe. He studied Bio-Medical Engineering at the University of Utah; however, his love for stories and storytelling took him down a different career path. When he's not writing he enjoys spending time with his wife and daughters, playing video games, practicing martial arts and immersing himself in a good story.

Lightning Source UK Ltd.
Milton Keynes UK
UKHW010014270721
387818UK00007B/466/J